"Hurry, Mike, or the boat will be gone."

Samantha rushed up to Mike and grabbed his arm. "Quick, light the bonfire—we can signal the boat."

He swung around to face her and spoke with bewildering urgency. "Let it go, Sam," he said. "Why go back to civilization when we're happy and content as we are? We have each other...."

She stared at him in stunned surprise.

"But we can't stay here forever, Mike!"

"No, not forever, but there'll be other boats. We can wait for the next one, or the one after that."

"There might not be another boat for months," Sam cried. "Oh, Mike, please! We have to light the bonfire."

Relunctantly he lifted the red-hot brand and carried it toward the pile of coconut fiber and driftwood. "Oh, Sam," he said in a strange, cracked voice, "if you only knew what you are doing...."

Other titles by

SALLY WENTWORTH
IN HARLEQUIN ROMANCES

SALLY WENTWORTH

candle in the wind

Harlequin Books

TORONTO • LONDON • NEW YORK • AMSTERDAM
SYDNEY • HAMBURG • PARIS • STOCKHOLM

Harlequin Presents edition published July 1980
ISBN 0-373-10372-7

Original hardcover edition published in 1979
by Mills & Boon Limited

CHAPTER ONE

THE first thing she remembered was pain—a sharp, tearing pain that shot through her head and made her clench her teeth in agony. It continued for some time, but gradually lessened to a persistent, throbbing ache so long as she lay very still and didn't try to move. Slowly other senses began to return and she realised that she was lying on something hard and wooden, something that seemed to be moving slightly of its own volition. It was a long time before she tried to open her eyes, and when she did so she was gripped with sheer, overwhelming panic. Because she could see nothing, there was only impenetrable blackness all around her, suffocating her like a blanket, and she knew with sickening realisation that she must be blind. Desperately she turned her head, eyes probing for even a pinprick of light, of colour, to break up the darkness, anything to prove her wrong. Turning her head gave her light and colour all right, great shooting, spiked rockets of them, but inside her head, not outside, and the pain made her cry out in anguish.

Immediately the floor began to heave and tilt beneath her and she gave a gasp of fear. Then, for the first time, sounds came to break the enveloping silence, sounds that came nearer as the floor rocked more violently. A hand touched her ankle and then moved up her body, and she could hear someone breathing softly. Her eyes probed the blackness, wide and frightened. If only she could see! The hand found her shoulder and then touched the cold skin of her face. With a cry of sheer terror she dropped back into the blessedness of oblivion.

When next she came to she was afraid to open her eyes at first, afraid that there would only be blackness again, but eventually hope that she might have been mistaken overcame her fears and she lifted her lids. Immediately a great wave of relief swept over her; no longer was everything pitch black, now it was grey, a dark, uniform grey, admittedly, but the upsurge of hope it gave her was tremendous. For a few moments she lay still, too thankful to think of anything else, but then she became aware of the throbbing ache in her head. Tentatively she lifted her hand to touch it and then stopped in surprise as she felt the dressing just above her right temple. Slowly her fingers explored it. She must have hurt her head and someone had dressed it for her. Who? Who was it? She tried to speak, to call out, but her throat felt dry and parched and she only managed a feeble moan.

But it was enough. The floor began to move as it had before and the sounds came again. She remembered then the hand that had touched her and she grew rigid with apprehension, waiting. But the sounds were surer this time, less fumbling, and suddenly the greyness above her was lifted and for a moment her eyes were dazzled by brilliant sunlight. Instinctively she closed them against it, but then the light was blotted out as someone leaned over her. She found herself being lifted gently into a sitting position and then a voice said, 'Here, drink this.'

It was a man. He was holding a water bottle to her

lips and she bent to drink it greedily, but he made her take only a few sips at first, until her throat was lubricated and she could swallow properly, then he let her drink as much as she wanted. Afterwards he laid her down again and checked the dressing on her head and felt her pulse, his fingers hot against her skin. He seemed satisfied and moved away. Then the greyness came down again and she realised that it was a cover he had spread over her to protect her from the sun.

She slept again then, a deep, reviving sleep, and when she woke the pain in her head was almost gone, leaving only the aftermath of a severe headache. It was much cooler now, the heat seemed to have gone out of the sun, and when she looked up she could see the pale grey of the sky above her. Gingerly she lifted her head and with a shock of surprise realised that she was in a boat, a wooden dinghy that moved gently with the waves. The blanket had been wrapped round her, but despite its warmth she shivered. The air was cold and she realised that it was very early in the morning, the sun not yet having risen.

Painfully she raised herself a little further, her limbs stiff and cramped from having lain still for so long. The man was at the other end of the boat, half lying, half sitting against the side, his head pillowed on his arm, asleep. Because of his position she couldn't see his face very well, and it was impossible to tell whether or not he was tall, but she got the impression that he was a big man, his broad shoulders making the boat seem too small for him. On the horizon the grey sky began to turn to a rich pink as the sun slowly crept towards them. Pulling herself upright, she settled herself as comfortably as she could and waited for the man to waken.

He did so as the first rays of sunlight caught him, stretching his cramped muscles and putting a rueful hand to his unshaven face. Then he became aware that she was watching him. For a moment he studied her, and she saw that his eyes were deep blue like the sea. Easing himself forward, he sat on the seat opposite her. His eyes crinkled into a smile. 'Hi, how's the head?'

'All right.' She looked at him anxiously. 'Please— why are we on this boat?'

'Don't you remember? The boat we were on capsized in a storm. You banged your head against something and were knocked unconscious. There was just time to get you into the dinghy before she went down.'

She looked at him in bewilderment. 'What about the other people?'

He frowned. 'There were no other people—just the two of us.'

Her eyebrows drew together in puzzlement. 'But I ...' She paused, then said questioningly, 'Who are you?'

He stared at her, completely taken aback, and he didn't answer for what seemed a long time. Then he leaned forward and looked at her searchingly.

'I'm Mike. Mike Scott. Don't you remember? We were on my boat together, the *Venturer*.'

Slowly she shook her head. 'No, I'm sorry, I—I can't seem to remember.' She lifted her hand to the wound on her temple as the pain began to come back. 'My head, it hurts so!'

He put a hand on her shoulder. 'Don't worry about it now, Sam, you'll probably be ...'

She raised her head to look at him. 'Who's Sam?'

His eyes flew wide in his suddenly taut face and the hand gripping her shoulder tightened so that his fingers bit into her flesh and she winced.

'Don't you know?' His voice was sharp, urgent.

'No.' She was bewildered and a little frightened by his tone.

He continued to gaze at her for several minutes, then he said curiously, 'Can't you remember—anything?'

And then she knew. Tears filled her eyes and she cried out. 'No! Oh, no!' Desperately she pressed her hands against her head and tried to go back, back. But there was nothing there, only a deep impenetrable black void that left her without name and identity. She balled her hands into fists and began to beat them against her forehead, trying to force herself to remember.

'Sam, stop it. You'll hurt yourself!'

He grabbed hold of her flailing wrists and the next second she was pulled roughly against him and held close in his arms as he knelt in the bottom of the boat. Tears of anguish and fear ran down her cheeks and her body shook with emotion. Putting up a hand, he held her head against his shoulder.

'Cry it out, sweetheart. Let it go.'

And he just held her for a long time, until her sobs had quietened and she wasn't shaking quite so violently. Then he loosened his hold a little so that he could look down at her.

Gently he said, 'Your name is Sam. You've been hit on the head and it's made you forget who you are for the moment, that's all. Nothing unusual about that, it often happens with bangs on the head. It will probably all start coming back to you in a day or so, when you get better. But not if you keep worrying about it.' He gently put up a hand to cup her chin. 'So promise me you'll try not to worry.'

Still held within the circle of his arm, she answered falteringly, 'All—all right, I'll try. But I . . .'

He put a finger against her lips. 'Hush, that's good enough for now. You'll make your head hurt again.'

'But, please, I have to know who I am. Who you are?'

He hesitated for a moment, and his eyes darkened. Then he said firmly, 'You're my wife.'

He let her go then and made her sit in the prow of the boat while he rigged the blanket over her as a shelter from the sun again, then he gave her a drink of water.

'Not too much this time,' he warned her. 'It's all we have and we don't know how long it will have to last us.'

She obeyed him meekly and then sat staring out across the empty sea unseeingly. Her name was Sam— short for Samantha, she supposed. And this man was her husband, the man who shared her life. What had he said his name was? Mike, that was it. Mike Scott. She watched him as he took a small drink of water from the plastic container and then stowed it under the seat out of the sun. Taking a pair of oars that she hadn't noticed before from the bottom of the boat, he fitted them into the rowlocks and began to row, steering a course from the sun.

The hands that held the oars were strong, capable, and his muscles rippled under the blue sweat shirt he wore as he rowed without apparent effort. Almost surreptitiously she studied his face. He was very tanned, his thick brown hair bleached to a lighter shade by the sun, and he had square, masterful features that made him look tough and immensely self-assured, but there was a slight ironic quirk to his mouth as if he laughed at himself and other people too much. Everything about him suggested a casual, easy approach to life, an 'I don't give a damn' manner. The blue eyes flickered over her for a moment and she looked away quickly.

There was nothing to see all around her, only the deep blue of the sea and the azure of the cloudless sky. For the first time it hit home to her that they were in a very small boat on a very big sea. She tried to think where they were, where the boat had been heading before it sank, but there was still nothing there, nothing before the pain she had woken to—like the pain of being born? she wondered. Hesitatingly she turned to address the man—no, not the man, her husband. She bit her lip. Oh, why couldn't she remember? Why?

After a minute she said slowly, 'Please, where are we?'

He grinned. 'I've been wondering when you'd get round to asking me that. We're somewhere in the Caribbean Sea and heading towards the Windward Islands. How far away they are I'm not sure exactly, we got swept along quite a way during the storm. But if we keep heading west we're bound to hit land eventually, even if it's the coast of America.'

'Is there—is there anything to eat?'

For a moment his eyes were shadowed. 'Sorry, Sam, but the boat went down so fast I didn't have time to grab more than the water and the first aid kit after I'd . . .' He stopped and gave her a reassuring grin. 'But don't worry, we'll make it—we haven't come this far not to survive the rest.'

He bent to the oars and Sam was left to her thoughts. In the Caribbean, he'd said, heading for the Windward Islands. She was surprised to find that she knew what he was talking about. The Windward Islands were in the West Indies. So if she could remember something like that why couldn't she remember anything else? She tried, forcing her mind back to the brink of the abyss but finding only emptiness beyond it. It was as if someone had pulled down a blind and shut everything out. After a little while she gave up, it made her head ache painfully whenever she tried to concentrate too much and already there were red flashes before her eyes. She shut them and leaned back against the side of the boat. So they were adrift in a small boat with only a little water between them. And the sun beating down on them, its rays already so hot that they burned through the blanket that shaded her. It came to her then that she might die without knowing who she was.

They rowed on in silence, Mike concentrating all his strength in pulling the oars like a robot. In, out, in, out. But as the day wore on, his breathing rasped in his throat and sweat trickled down his face and stained his shirt. She watched him, wanting to cry out to him to stop, to rest, but knowing instinctively that for all his reassurance their plight was desperate. How long could they possibly survive in these conditions unless they found land? Only when the sun was high in the sky did he at last stop, leaning on the oars, his breathing laboured. Slowly he shipped the oars and then pulled off his shirt to wash it in the sea. He was very strong, his shoulders wide and powerful, and there was a mat of hair on his chest which was tanned as brown as his face.

He spread the shirt to dry and then looked over at her. 'Mind if I share your shade for a bit?'

Bringing the water container with him, he let her drink first and then took some himself. No more than a swallow, although he must have been completely dehydrated. Then he lay down in the bottom of the boat and looked at her as she sat rather stiffly beside him.

'Might as well try and get some sleep during the heat of the day. I'll row again later when it's cooled down.'

'What if we drift in the wrong direction?'

A look of amusement appeared in the blue eyes. 'We won't. The current is carrying us the way we want to go all the time.'

'But what if we go past an island while we're asleep?' she objected.

'Look around you,' he instructed her. 'What do you see?'

'Nothing. Nothing at all.'

'No, and even if there was land in sight it would take us hours to reach it and we'd be awake long before then. You don't have to worry, Sam,' he said quietly. 'I won't let anything happen to you, not now I've got you. Now come and get some sleep.'

Slowly she slid down beside him and he put an arm under her head as a pillow. His other arm he put casually across her, just above her waist. He did it quite naturally, as if he was used to having her body close up against his like this. She could feel the hairs on his chest soft against her bare arm, feel his heart beating strongly against her shoulder. Sam lay there, rigidly still, unable to relax, let alone think of sleep. It felt so strange, so alien, to lie beside him like this, she was tinglingly aware of every place where his body touched hers: her shoulder, her arm, her hip, her leg. Why was it that she couldn't remember something that set her nerves jangling like this? Surely she should remember how it was when he made love to her, when he laid her slim body under his big one and possessed her completely?

The thought made her quiver and his arm tightened around her.

'Relax. Try and sleep,' he said softly in her ear.

She tried, but it was no good. There were too many things she had to know. Taking her courage in both hands, she said falteringly, 'How long have we been married?'

He didn't answer immediately, then said almost dismissively, 'Not long. Go to sleep.'

But she persisted. 'Please—how long?'

Again he hesitated, then, reluctantly, 'About a week.'

'A week!' She turned startled eyes to stare at him.

He sighed, a little exasperatedly. 'We were on our honeymoon. We were married in Barbados and were going on a cruise round the islands.' He bunched his hand into a fist and gave her a mock blow on the chin. 'Now will you go to sleep, woman, or do I have to knock you unconscious again?'

So Sam subsided into silence, her thoughts chaotic. No wonder it felt strange, if they had only been married a week. And yet he acted so naturally. Perhaps it was different for a man. His breathing became rhythmic and even as he fell into an exhausted sleep and she sneaked a look at his face, so near her own. His features were hard, even in repose, only the sweep of his long eyelashes giving any softness to his face. For a long time she studied him, trying to find within herself the feelings she knew she ought to have for this man. But there was nothing there, only her awareness of him as a man, and her shyness and embarrassment at being so close to him. She wondered miserably if amnesia made you forget not only memories but feelings and emotions as well. Surely if she loved him she would still feel it? She moved restlessly and he murmured in his sleep, tightening his hold on her and burying his face in her hair, so that she was afraid to move lest she wake him, and eventually drifted off to sleep herself.

The worst of the heat had gone out of the sun when his stirring woke her. Her first reaction on waking was to send her mind searching back into her brain in the eager hope of her memory having returned, but there was still nothing there and Sam hastily reverted to the present, away from the pain of deep concentration. Beside her Mike sat up and flexed his stiff muscles, rubbing circulation back into the arm she had been lying on. He glanced up at the sky and grimaced.

'Not a cloud in sight, and no wind to speak of either, unfortunately.' He stood up, and to Sam's dismay began to unbuckle the belt of the jeans he was wearing. He glanced at her and said quite matter-of-factly, 'I'm going over the side for a swim.'

Her eyes widened in alarm. 'But isn't that dangerous? What if you can't get back in again, or the boat drifts away?'

'Don't worry, nothing's going to happen.'

He kicked off his deck shoes and began to take off his trousers and Sam looked away, studying the horizon on the other side of the boat unseeingly. The boat rocked violently and she caught hold of the side to steady herself. Anxiety made her turn to make sure that he was all right and she felt a great surge of relief when she saw his head break the surface a few yards away. He splashed around for about five minutes and then swam back to where she knelt at the side of the boat, watching him.

'Better hold on,' he told her. 'The boat will tip quite a bit.'

Putting his hands on the side, he gave one heave of his powerful shoulders that lifted him high out of the water, and the next second he was safely back on board, the water running in rivulets down his broad chest and strong legs. His underpants clung wetly to him and Sam hastily averted her eyes, her cheeks flushed with embarrassment. He turned to pick up his shirt and dry himself on it and several drops of water splashed on to her arm. They felt infinitely cool against her parched skin.

'Your turn now,' Mike said to her.

Sam stared at him. 'Oh, but I—I can't!' Her mind filled with fear at the thought of going into that vast empty sea.

'Why not?'

Her voice rose. 'I—I just can't, that's all.'

He came to sit opposite her. His hair was wet and drops of moisture still clung to the hairs on his chest. He seemed to loom over her, big and dominantly masculine, and Sam instinctively flinched away. His eyes narrowed but he spoke gently enough.

'Sam, you'll feel a whole lot better after you've been over the side and had a dip. You'll feel cooler and less dehydrated.'

She looked up at him unhappily. 'But I can't swim.'

His eyebrows flew up in astonishment. 'Sure you can. You swim like a fish.'

'No, I can't—I know I can't. I've forgotten how.'

His hand came up to stroke her arm gently and her flesh quivered under his touch. 'Once you get in the water it will probably all come back to you, it's one of those things that once you've learnt you can never forget. Now, come on,' he said more firmly, as if he was dealing with a recalcitrant child, 'you've been on this boat for two days and you need to take a dip. Here, I'll help you.'

His hand went to the waistband of her white denims, but she hastily stopped him. 'No! I—I can manage.' Fumblingly she reached down to take off her shoes and then undid the button at the waist of her jeans, but hesitated over the zip. He was still watching her. Her voice rose sharply. 'Must you sit there and look at me? You might at least turn your back.'

His jaw tightened. 'We're married, remember. It isn't the first time you've undressed in front of me. And the name's Mike,' he added on a hard note. 'But if that's what you want, you only have to ask.' And he turned and sat with his back to her.

Biting her lip, Sam took off her jeans and then went to unhook the halter-neck sun-top she was wearing, but found to her consternation that she wasn't wearing a bra underneath. Now what was she going to do? She glared at Mike's bare back and thought rather resentfully that it was all right for a man, but no way was she going over the side in just a pair of flimsy panties. After a moment she said in a faltering voice, 'I'm ready.'

'Okay, come on.' Mike glanced at her and his lip curled a little when he saw that she was still half dressed. He stood up and braced his legs in the boat, then put his hands on her slim waist and lifted her bodily over the side to lower her in the sea.

But Sam clung to him and wouldn't let go. 'No, I've changed my mind. I don't want to go in!' Her voice rose in a panic and she gripped his arms so tightly that she made marks in his flesh. The water came up her legs and she cried out in fear. 'You'll let me go. I'll drown!'

'No, I won't. Sam, trust me!'

His tone was insistent, compelling, and Sam looked deep into his eyes so near her own. Slowly the fear subsided a little and she didn't struggle any more as he lowered her gently into the water, keeping a firm hold on her arms. The sea lapped round her, luxuriously cool and reviving against her burning skin. The waves lifted her, dragging her away from the boat, but Mike kept a tight grip on her wrists. Gradually her fears diminished, but she was still afraid to trust herself to the water alone, she knew that without Mike holding her she would sink like a stone.

'Okay?' he asked, and when she nodded lifted her easily out and back into the boat.

Water cascaded off her and made her clothes transparent. She might as well not have been wearing anything at all.

He handed her his shirt. 'Here, dry yourself with this.' Deliberately he turned his back.

Sam raised the shirt to wipe her face and then her hands slowed. She had made him angry and he was more like a stranger than ever. Haltingly she said, 'I'm sorry. Please don't be angry with me.' Then tentatively, 'Mike?'

He turned to look at her over his shoulder, a crooked grin on his lips. 'I'm sorry too. I should have realised and made allowances. I guess it's going to take us both a little time to adjust.' The grin deepened. 'But at least you called me by my name.'

Her clothes dried on her almost at once and she was able to put her jeans back on, turning away while Mike, too, dressed. Then they had a drink of water, and Sam noticed with misgivings that the canister was now less than half full.

'How much longer will it last, do you think?' she asked anxiously.

He shrugged non-committally. 'There's plenty there. And if it rains we can fill it up. As soon as the sun goes down I'll row again.'

They settled themselves under the blanket to wait. Mike's arm lay negligently along the side of the boat and for a while Sam sat stiffly, something inside her unwilling for any physical contact with him, but gradually she relaxed and leaned back against his arm, and presently he moved to pillow her head more comfortably against his shoulder, but he didn't say anything.

After a while she said questioningly, 'Mike, did you manage to rescue our passports?'

There was a sudden tenseness in him that she could feel and it was a moment before he answered. 'No, there wasn't time. Why?'

'I—I wanted to look at the photograph. I wondered what I looked like.'

Immediately the tenseness eased and he put up his other hand to turn her face towards him. His blue eyes under their rather heavy lids scanned her face, studying each feature as if imprinting them for ever in his mind.

'You're very, very lovely,' he said, and then he bent his head and kissed her. His lips were hard and firm and tasted of salt. His two-day growth of beard scratched her skin, but she was hardly aware of it. For a few moments she was surprised by his action and her lips were soft and yielding under his, but then he felt her stiffen under his touch, become tense and fearful. Immediately he released her. Sam started to speak, but he stopped her, a finger against her quivering lips. His face was expressionless as he said brusquely, 'Your eyes are hazel and your hair's brunette, with a sort of chestnut glow to it. You look ...' his eyes settled on her again and his voice became more gentle, 'you look okay.'

Slowly Sam went over what he'd said. She put up a hand to feel her hair and found that it was quite short and curly; she tried to pull a few strands forward and squint sideways at them, but it didn't tell her very much. Then she explored her face with her fingers, much as a blind person would, trying to find out more. Her nose was straight, her mouth even with a slightly fuller lower lip, and her eyebrows felt as if they arched slightly. And hazel eyes, he'd said. Did that add up to very, very lovely? She remembered the sudden flare in his eyes as he'd bent to kiss her, the firmness of his mouth on hers. Had he really expected her to respond? Presumably he had, if she was his wife. But there was no 'if' about it. She *was* his wife, albeit a very, very new one. She just had to get used to the idea and try not to be so on edge with him. For a moment she tried to put herself in his place; it must be very hard for him too, to go from having a loving bride one minute and then to be treated like a complete stranger the next.

Sam stole a glance at Mike under her lashes and found him watching her with a rather brooding expression in his eyes. This changed as soon as he realised she was looking at him and he said, 'The sun's low enough, I'll row again now.'

Moving to the other end of the boat, he bent to the oars as the sun began its descent through the empty sky. He rowed steadily for over an hour, seemingly tireless, but then he stopped to rest. Ruefully he looked down at his hands and then took a penknife from his pocket and cut some strips from the bottom of his shirt and started to wrap them round the palms of his hands.

'Are your hands very sore? Here, let me see.'

Sam got up to go to him, but he said sharply, 'Stay where you are. It's just to avoid getting blisters, that's all.'

Feeling strangely rebuffed, Sam subsided into her seat again. She felt hot and thirsty, even though the heat had gone out of the sun. Her mouth was parched and she longed for a drink of water. Mike picked up the oars and began to row once more. The sun dropped to the horizon, turning the sky to a brilliant, molten red that lightened to orange above before it sank and was gone, leaving them alone in the darkness of the empty sea.

The next day was much as before; they both went over the side to wash themselves, although Sam didn't feel any more confident than she had before and still clung to Mike's hands. He allowed them just a mouthful of water each three times during the course of the long day. They rested during the hottest part, huddled under the meagre shade of the blanket, and they didn't talk much, their throats were too dry and swollen, and besides, there didn't seem to be much to say, although Sam did rouse herself sufficiently to ask a question that had suddenly become important.

'Mike, will you tell me about my family? I—I'd like to know.'

There was a long wait before he said in a harsh, terse voice, 'You have no family.'

Appalled, she turned to look at him where he lay so close beside her. 'No one? No one at all?'

'You have me.' Almost roughly he pulled her to him and held her head against his shoulder. 'Don't think about it, Sam. Nothing that happened to you before we got married matters any more.'

The thought crossed her mind that it was a strange thing to say, but the knowledge that she was completely alone in the world except for him put everything else out of her head. She suddenly felt very lonely. There was no one to care that she was adrift in this small boat with only a little water left between life and a certain death under the scorching rays of the sun. Listlessly she lay there until she fell into a fitful sleep in which nightmares chased one another and she woke with a start to find herself again in that pitch black part of the night before the moon had risen. The only sounds were of the waves lapping gently against the boat and she was suddenly filled with dread.

'Mike!' Her voice was sharp with terrified fear as she groped around to try and find him but could feel nothing but the familiar sides of the boat.

'I'm here.' His voice came, low and tired from the

other end of the boat, and tears of relief splashed down her face. 'What is it?'

'I—I couldn't find you. I was afraid that you—that you . . .'

'I'm all right.' His tone was short, abrupt. 'Go back to sleep.'

He had put the blanket over her and she pulled it closer. For a while she was silent, then she said with difficulty, 'We're not going to make it, are we?'

When he answered his voice was derisive. 'Don't give up so easily, Sam. There's plenty of life in us yet. I didn't spend weeks chasing after you to lose you as soon as I'd married you.'

'Did you? Chase me, I mean.'

He laughed. It was a croaking, wheezing effort, but it was definitely a laugh. 'Like a lovesick tomcat. Don't worry, sweetheart, we'll make it.'

Sam lay back, immeasurably heartened, but as the next day passed without any sign of land, not even a seabird, hope began to diminish again. Mike rowed like an automaton, but his strokes were less powerful and he had to stop frequently to rest. Once he cut off some of the stronger material from the legs of his jeans to replace that bound round his hands. He tried to keep the old bindings from her sight, but to Sam's horror she saw that they were bright with blood.

'Oh, Mike, your hands! Your poor hands!'

'It's nothing.' His voice was gruff. 'But I won't be able to go over the side today, and when I hold you I'll have to keep my hands out of the water.'

She looked bewildered. 'Why?'

'The scent of blood attracts sharks. We'd have a pack of them round us in a minute.'

He held her over the side, keeping his hands high out of the sea, but when he tried to pull her back it took him a long time and when he at last managed it they were both exhausted, lying haphazardly in the bottom of the boat, their breathing laboured in their constricted throats.

'Time for a drink,' Mike managed at last. He groped for the canister. 'Here.' There was only about half an inch left in it.

Sam lifted it to her lips and drank slowly, greedily savouring each drop as it trickled down her parched throat.

'That's enough.'

Reluctantly she gave it back and Mike screwed on the stopper.

'But you haven't had any.'

'I'm not thirsty.'

'But you must be. Mike, please!'

'I'll drink later when it's cool. I'd only lose it in sweat when I'm rowing.'

He went back to the other end of the boat and Sam dropped back into sleep. She awoke from time to time but was now so completely enervated that her mind became disorientated and she was only vaguely aware of the passage of time. She felt the coolness of the night and then the heat of another day, but she had no strength left to move, had lost the hope of ever seeing land. Once she opened her eyes and found Mike above her. He lifted her head and poured some water down her throat. It tasted warm and brackish, but she gulped at it till she'd painfully swallowed the last drop. Her lips formed the word, 'More,' but he shook his head.

She heard him whisper croakingly, 'It's all gone.' He

lay down beside her and took her gently in his arms, his hands leaving bloodstains on her clothes. She felt his dry lips touch hers for a moment and then the whisper came again. 'Sorry, Sam. I tried ... God, how I tried.' But then she slipped back into semi-consciousness.

It was the cold that woke her—an intense, penetrating cold that made her shiver convulsively. A strong breeze ruffled her hair and made the waves bang noisily against the boat. The sea sounded so loud in her ears. Feebly Sam pulled herself up, holding on to the side. The wind hit her more fiercely now and she was so weak that it almost knocked her down again, but she managed to keep hold of the rowlock and turned to look out. The boat was pitching wildly as large waves tossed it over the sea like a piece of straw. The tops of the waves were capped with white and spray splashed against her face and blinded her for a few seconds. Feebly she wiped her eyes. The first rays of dawn were beginning to lighten the sky, but there were great clouds, dark and heavy with rain. Rain! If only the storm would break so that they could get a drink of water, fill up the container. Hope flickered in her and she stared up at the sky for what seemed a long time, but the wind merely got stronger and drove them away from the rain clouds while the sound of the waves became even louder in her ears and despair filled her heart again.

It was several minutes before she realised that what she heard was the crash of breakers against something solid. Quickly she turned to look over the prow of the boat and then froze in astonishment. Only a short distance ahead of them she could see where the waves spewed up great sheets of spray as they thundered against the jagged rocks of a reef—and beyond the reef, silhouetted against the golden dawning of the sun, there was land! A land of hills and trees, of water and life!

Recovering from her stupefaction, she leant down to Mike and began to shake him frenziedly. 'Mike! Mike, wake up! Oh, please wake up. There's land. Land! We're safe!' But he didn't stir and the sudden realisation hit her that he might be dead. 'No! Oh, no!' She shook him again, so hard that his head bumped against the wooden boards of the boat.

He gave a groan and tried feebly to turn his head away.

'Mike! Wake up!' Sam was almost yelling in his ear, against the noise of the breakers.

Opening his eyes at last, he stared up at her. 'Sam?'

'It's land! We made it, Mike, we made it!'

He pulled himself up and looked over the side, then his shoulders stiffened. Sam followed his gaze and then stared in fascinated horror. The boat was heading straight for the thick band of the reef, its jagged rocks rearing out of the water like the teeth of a shark, ready to take their frail little boat and tear it to pieces. They had found land, but they were by no means safe, they still hadn't made it.

As the boat was thrown towards the reef, Mike turned and grabbed the blanket and began to wrap it round her. 'Don't hold on to the boat,' he shouted at her above the roar. 'Let the waves take you.' He put his arms round her and locked his wrists into a tight grip. 'Here it comes!' He pulled her on top of him and braced himself against the prow of the dinghy.

Sam put her arms round his neck and clung to him. 'Mike, I'm afraid. Don't let me go.'

The last thing she heard him say before the boat hit the reef and started to disintegrate under them was said strongly and firmly, 'I'll never let you go.' And then the water closed over their heads as they were dragged into the boiling maelstrom of the sea.

CHAPTER TWO

SAM lay on the beach, gasping and retching, as Mike knelt over her and unrelentingly pumped the water out of her lungs until he was sure that she was all right. Only then did he collapse beside her, his breathing laboured. They lay immobile for a long time, just above the water's edge, completely oblivious of their surroundings, just thankful to be alive and on land, and spent and exhausted by the struggle to get ashore. And it was a struggle that Sam would certainly have lost on her own. She remembered being thrown against the rocks and the coral heads tearing at the blanket and scraping her skin, of being pulled down by the current no matter how hard she tried to fight it and her lungs bursting in her chest until Mike had lifted her up, up to the surface and she could breathe again, great, wonderful gulps of air. But then they had been sucked under once more by a cruel twist of the current and the fight had started all over again, and this time she had swallowed water and been near to drowning when he pulled her out.

As they lay stretched out on the beach the sun grew higher in the sky, warming them and drying their clothes, but its heat also brought thirst back to torment them. Mike woke first and sat up slowly. Then he bent to shake her.

'Sam, wake up! Come on. We have to find water.' His voice was hoarse in his dry throat.

She didn't move at first, but he persisted and at last she stirred and tried to jerk away from him, unwilling to wake from the deep sleep that bordered on semi-consciousness.

'Come on, Sam. Get up!' He pulled her to her knees and shook her.

'No. Leave me alone,' she mumbled, and tried to lie down again.

'Just a bit more effort, sweetheart, then you can rest again. But first we have to find water.'

'Water?'

The word brought her more awake and she managed to stay standing up when he got her on her feet.

'Yes, we have to go and find it.' Mike put his arm round her and half dragged her along the beach as he looked for a river or stream flowing into the sea.

The beach was long and white with palm trees growing almost to the water's edge in some places. Exotic seashells lay littered on the sand and here and there a crab would scuttle to its hole as they passed. Mike looked hopefully round for signs of habitation, but there was no trace of any huts, no boats drawn up on the beach, nothing to say whether the island was inhabited. The beach went on endlessly and they had gone for nearly half a mile with no trace of fresh water and Sam sagged against Mike, what little strength she had completely exhausted.

'So tired ... must rest,' she croaked, and almost fell asleep leaning against him.

'No, you've got to keep going. I can't bring the water to you, you've got to walk.' He shook her hard, but she hardly opened her eyes and started to sink to her knees as soon as he let go. Propping her up with one shoulder, Mike raised his hand and hit her across the face, twice, with all his strength. It wasn't hard, he was too weak to really hurt her, but it made Sam jerk awake and stare at him out of large, puzzled eyes.

'Now, come on. If you fall down you'll die, do you hear me, you'll die!' He tried to shout at her, to make his voice harsh, but it came out as only a hoarse whisper. But there was a fierce anger in his eyes, and this and his words got through to her. Somehow she pulled herself upright and turned to go on up the beach, concentrating on her feet and willing them to move forward and take another step and then another, until she was moving like a zombie, her mind empty of anything but the effort she was making.

She never knew how far they walked, it seemed like a hundred miles but might have been only a few hundred yards before Mike put a hand on her arm and stopped her. He said something, but Sam didn't hear. With the impetus to keep moving suddenly taken from her, she dropped to the sand like a stone and she was unconscious even before she hit the ground.

The next thing she remembered was having something wet put between her lips and precious drops of water trickling slowly into her throat. This happened regularly until at last she could swallow again and then she was given a proper drink. She opened her eyes and saw Mike bending over her, and above their heads the shady leaves of a casuarina tree sheltered them from the sun's glare. She gave him a weak smile and he grinned back at her before lying down beside her and pillowing her head on his shoulder and going to sleep.

When next Sam woke she was able to sit up and look around her. They were in a large clearing in the woodland where rays of sunlight shafted down between the trees and made dappled patterns on the ground. She could hear the musical tinkle of water over stone, and when she looked to her left she saw a wide stream that flowed quite fast through the clearing. Mike was still fast asleep beside her and she gently eased herself up so as not to wake him. She drank long and deep of the cool, clean water, fresh as any mountain stream, and then splashed some over herself. Her skin felt so dry and she could still feel the salt from the sea on it and in her hair. She glanced hesitantly at Mike; he was still in a deep sleep, but supposing he woke? For a moment longer she hesitated, then started to walk along beside the stream, further inland. Past the clearing the vegetation closed in again and among the trees there grew exotic flowers, wild hibiscus, oleander and ginger lilies, and almost smothering the trees were vines of morning glory and purple bougainvillaea. Humming birds, their wings vibrating so fast that they became invisible, flitted through the trees and hovered by the fragrant blossoms. Sam stood quite still and watched them for a little while, fascinated, until she realised with a little shock that she knew the names of the flowers and the birds. Was her memory coming back, or was it just another of those strange twists of her brain which let her remember general things but nothing about herself?

The noise of the stream got louder as she went further on and presently she came to a pool where a waterfall jutted out from a rock face about ten feet high. Quickly she slipped out of her clothes and washed them as best she could in the pool, then spread them out to dry in a patch of sunlight. She stepped into the pool, it wasn't deep, only up to her knees, and waded towards the waterfall. The water struck very cold and made her gasp at first, but then she lifted her face towards it and gave herself up to the pure bliss of having it pour over her, just revelling in the deliciously invigorating feel of it against her dry, parched skin. After a while she began to wash herself, wishing she had some soap and a shampoo for her hair, but at least she felt clean again. Wading out of the pool, she stood in a shaft of sunlight to dry off, using her fingers as combs to get the tangles out of her hair. The sun was so hot that she was soon dry and bent to feel her clothes. Her pants were nylon and were quite dry, but the sun-top was still a little damp and her jeans were so thick that they would take quite a while. Bending down, Sam stepped into her pants and then whirled round as she heard a noise behind her.

Mike had come to find her. He pushed aside a branch of a frangipani tree and came towards her. Instinctively Sam's hands flew up to cover her bare breasts. His eyes ran over her and his mouth twisted a little, but then he looked at the waterfall.

'That looks good. Think I'll join you.'

He bent to take off his shoes and Sam turned to put on her top, even though it was still damp, carefully keeping her back towards him. She pretended to examine her jeans again and presently she heard him splashing through the pool. Sitting down on the grass, she lifted up her hair to let the sun dry it, but then gave a little smile as she heard Mike begin to whistle behind her. Nothing seemed to get him down, he had an immense fortitude and will-power; if it hadn't been for him ... Sam shivered as she recalled the danger they had been in. She owed her life to him several times over and she would always be grateful, but she still didn't feel completely at ease with him even though they had been living in such intimate closeness for several days. She heard him come out of the water and begin to dress and she hastily pulled on her jeans.

'Mm, that's better. How do you feel, Sam?' His voice had lost its hoarseness and was firm and strong again.

Hesitantly she turned round to find him putting on his shoes. He had on his denims but his chest was bare. His days on the boat had deepened his tan and he was very brown. It suited him, he was the outdoor type.

'I'm fine, thanks to you.'

He straightened up and crossed to her. 'You certainly look a whole lot better. More like the girl I married,' he added deliberately.

Sam flushed and moved away, but he came up behind her and put his hands on her bare waist.

His mouth was very close to her ear as he said, 'Sam, don't be shy. You don't have to cover yourself in front of me.'

'I—I know, but I can't help it.' She bit her lip and turned her head away.

'Sweetheart.' His lips were burning hot against her skin as he bent to kiss her shoulder and then his hands came up to cup her breasts.

She jerked away from him and turned like an animal at bay.

Mike's eyes darkened for a moment and then he gave a rueful shake of his head. 'Sorry, Sam.' He held out his hand. 'Let's go and see if we can find something to eat, shall we?'

After a moment she put her hand in his and he led her back along the stream towards the sea. They found food in plenty: small plantains that were sweeter than cultivated bananas, figs, breadfruit and potatoes. They sat on the beach in the dying rays of the sun and ate their first meal in days. It tasted wonderful, but Sam soon found that she'd had enough because her stomach had shrunk and she couldn't manage more than two or three pieces of fruit and part of a raw potato.

'Don't worry,' Mike told her. 'You'll soon be back to normal and eating like a horse again.'

Sam was indignant. 'I don't eat like a horse.'

He grinned. 'Sure you do. I reckon it's going to take every penny I've got just to feed you.'

She smiled at his teasing, but then asked, 'What do you do, Mike? For a living, I mean?'

For a brief second his eyes glanced at her and then he looked away. 'What's the matter, afraid I won't be able to keep you in food? Don't worry, Sam, I'll provide.' He stood up and pulled her to her feet. 'Come on, we'd better find somewhere to spend the night where we won't be bothered by crabs.'

They found a hollow in the clearing by the stream and Mike used a broken coconut husk to deepen it and give them shelter from the night breeze. When it was ready he gave her no time for hesitation but drew her decisively down beside him and pulled the banana leaves he had cut over them before fitting her body into his and wrapping his arms round her. Sam tried to tell herself that it was just the same as on the dinghy, but there was a new tenseness between them that made her hold herself stiffly away from him until she fell asleep at last.

In the morning they breakfasted on coconut milk and wild bananas and then Mike suggested they walk back to where they had come ashore the previous day to see if they could find the boat. It had seemed a very long way before, but it took them only ten minutes to re- trace their footsteps through the sand. Of the dinghy they found only a few broken planks, but the blanket had been washed up by the tide and they saw the water container bobbing about in the sea a short distance away. They piled the planks together and then Mike put his hands on his hips and looked around him.

'No signs of life. Could be we're on an uninhabited island.'

Sam looked at him in some alarm. 'You mean we could be stranded here?'

He spoke reassuringly. 'For a short while, perhaps. But there's bound to be a boat within sight sooner or later.' He indicated a piece of higher ground visible above the trees. 'As soon as I can I'll climb up there and get a better look.'

Picking up some of the planks of wood he walked back towards the stream and Sam followed with the blanket and container. They were still so weak that even this small effort tired them and they were glad enough to sit down in the shade and rest.

They spent the rest of the day quietly, lying in the shade, eating and sleeping as they felt like it, but to- wards evening Mike caught a crab and tied the flesh to the end of a stripped piece of vine to use as bait when he waded into the lagoon to try and catch a fish. He came back triumphantly and then scooped a hole in the sand to use as an oven, making a fire by patiently rubbing two stones together and setting light to some dry coconut fibre. He gutted the fish and stuffed them with bananas before wrapping them in leaves and putting them in the makeshift oven.

Sam watched in fascination. 'Will you have to rub two stones together like that every time we want to cook something?'

'No, the oven will stay hot for a couple of days and we'll be able to get a flame from it.'

'You seem to know so much about it that I'd almost believe you'd been shipwrecked before,' Sam remarked.

He merely replied, 'I was a boy scout,' and Sam felt vaguely disappointed; he told her so little about himself.

She decided to be more direct, after all she had the right to know about him if she was his wife.

'How old are you, Mike?'

'So you're feeling well enough to ask questions again, are you? I'm thirty-five—and you're twenty-two.'

'How long have we known each other?'

He was concentrating on putting some breadfruit into the sand oven. 'Nearly three months.'

'Only three months? Is that all?'

He glanced at her briefly. 'It was long enough.'

Sam digested this for a minute and then asked, 'How did we meet?'

She thought she saw him hesitate, but then he said, 'We bumped into each other in Bridgetown one day.'

'Bridgetown?'

He sat back and looked at her. 'You don't remember that? It's the capital of Barbados.'

She shook her head. 'How strange. I know the names of flowers and birds, but I don't remember the name of a town. Did we both live there—in Bridgetown?'

Again he seemed to hesitate slightly. 'No, you lived further north and I lived on the boat.'

Sam gave a little sigh; it was obvious that he wasn't going to volunteer any information and she would just have to draw each item out of him.

'Did we intend to live in Bridgetown after we got back from—from our honeymoon?'

This time he answered immediately. 'No, we were going to just sail around the world until we found somewhere we liked and settle there for a while, then move on again.'

He busied himself with the oven again then and Sam was left to puzzle over the few scraps of information she had gained. So it seemed they had no settled home, that both of them were without any ties and were free to wander as they chose. But surely Mike must earn a living somehow? Then she remembered that she'd asked him that already and he had evaded an answer. It was all very puzzling and left a nagging seed of doubt and worry in her mind.

Mike broke into her thoughts. 'Dinner is served. How would madam like it, on a leaf or in a coconut shell?'

He was smiling at her, his eyes warm, and all doubts were pushed aside as she grinned back and responded in kind. 'In a coconut shell, of course. We'll use the leaves as napkins.'

Mike had used his penknife to shape pieces of driftwood into forks and they used these and shared the knife. The hot food tasted out of this world and made

them both feel almost back to normal again. Afterwards
Mike lay back and put his hands behind his head.

'Tomorrow I'll have a go at climbing that peak to
find out how big this island is.'

'Can I come with you?'

He gave a ghost of a smile. 'Sure, if you feel up to it.'

'I feel fine, especially after that lovely meal.' She
hesitated. 'Why did you smile when I asked you if I
could go with you?'

'Did I? I suppose it's because you seem to have
changed quite a lot since you got that bump on the
head. Before you wouldn't have asked, you'd just have
said, I'm coming with you.'

'Oh.' Sam didn't quite know how to take that. 'Do
you—do you mind that I've changed?'

He looked at her consideringly, head on one side,
while Sam waited in some trepidation, then he gave a
slow, crooked grin. 'I guess I could learn to live with it.
Come to think of it, I might even grow to like it.' He
glanced up at the sky, the deep red and mauve of sun-
set. 'The sun will go down shortly. We'd better get back
to the clearing before it gets dark.'

He banked more sand round the oven to retain the
heat and they followed the now familiar path alongside
the stream, reaching the clearing just as darkness fell.

'Might as well get some sleep; it could be a hard
climb tomorrow.'

They lay down in the hollow again and Mike pulled
the leaves over them, but he didn't draw her back
against him as he had the night before, instead he laid
her on her back and turned her face towards him. Then
he bent to kiss her. His lips were warm and gentle, for
the moment undemanding, but even so Sam immedi-

ately became tense and fearful. He must have felt it, but he went on kissing her for a little longer before he drew back and said quietly, 'Goodnight, Sam.'

Early the next morning they filled the container with water from the stream and set off to climb the hill before the day got too hot. They soon lost sight of the peak as the trees became denser, but Mike strode sure-footedly on, seeming to know by instinct which direction to take. The going was difficult because they had to climb over fallen tree trunks and push their way through the thick undergrowth, added to which they still hadn't completely recovered their strength. After an hour or so they stopped to rest and ate oranges from a nearby tree.

Sam watched a pair of bright yellow banana quits flying through the trees, calling shrilly to one another as they settled at last on a branch smothered in the dazzling colour of a morning glory vine. Sam leant back against the trunk of a tree and said dreamily, 'It's so beautiful and peaceful here.'

'Mm, I know what you mean. The West Indies are the nearest to paradise I've ever seen.'

'Have you travelled a lot?'

'Quite a bit. I used to go abroad on business.'

'You haven't always lived in Barbados, then?'

'No, I lived in England until about three years ago, then I came out here.' He stood up. 'If you're rested we'd better move on.'

After about another twenty minutes they broke free of the trees and began to climb over more rocky ground leading to the summit. It wasn't terribly high as hills go, but they were both out of breath by the time they got to the top, and Mike had had to help Sam up the

last few yards. She flopped down on to a rock to recover her breath while Mike shaded his eyes and looked
around.

'It's quite a small island, as I suspected. Not much
more than half a mile wide and about a mile long, I
should guess.'

Sam came to stand beside him as he examined the
coastline minutely. 'No signs of life, I'm afraid.'

'Look, over there!' Sam exclaimed as she pointed
to the northern horizon. 'Isn't that another island?'

They could just make out the darker outline of land
far away.

'It looks like it,' Mike agreed. 'Wonder what the horizon is from here; probably about fifty miles, I should
think.'

'Couldn't we send up a smoke signal, or something?'
Sam suggested eagerly. 'Then they could send a boat for
us.'

Mike shook his head regretfully. 'They'd never see it
from this distance. No, we'll either have to wait it out
here until we see a boat or a plane, or else try and
build some kind of boat or raft to take us across.'

'Where do you think we are?'

'On one of the Grenadines, I should think. That
whole range stretches for miles and is scattered with
little uninhabited islands like this, some of them not
much bigger than rocks. You often get charter yachts
bringing tourists to visit the lesser known islands, and
possibly natives come over now and again to cut down
some of the trees for timber. That's if they can get
through the reef, of course. Perhaps we'd better find out
if there's a gap in it anywhere and make camp near it,
so that we can be on hand if any boats do appear.'

They made their way back to the coast and Sam immediately took off her jeans and went into the sea to cool off. She was still half afraid of the water, it took some courage to try to swim and she went under once or twice, but suddenly it came back to her and she found herself doing an easy crawl through the water.

'I told you you could swim like a fish.'

Mike's voice made her turn and she saw him swimming towards her with long, powerful strokes. When he reached her he playfully splashed her and then laughingly moved out of the way when she tried to retaliate. He went on teasing her and Sam made a lot of noise, squealing with mock indignation and yelling threats at him.

'Just you wait, you bully!'

She managed to catch him at last and dived for his legs to pull him under for a minute. He twisted out of her grasp and came after her and Sam headed for the shore fast. Still laughing, she ran out of the water and turned to see him chasing after her, so she kept going up the beach, his footsteps flying behind her. He caught her after twenty yards and seized her wrist, pulling her round to face him, his eyes alight with laughter.

'Duck me, would you, you minx? There's only one punishment for that.'

Sam gave a shriek and tried to get away, but he held her easily and bent to pick her up and carry her back to the sea. She struggled against him, but he merely laughed at her and started to wade in.

'No, don't you dare duck me! Mike!'

Putting her arms round his neck, she clung on when he went to drop her so that she was leaning against him. Suddenly he stood still, and when Sam looked into his face she saw that the laughter had gone from his eyes, to be replaced by a kind of hunger. His arms tightened round her and he held her close against him.

'Sam. Oh, Sam, you're so lovely.'

He began to kiss her and this time his lips were hard and firm, demanding a response. Sam tried to pull away, but he wouldn't let her, increasing the pressure of his mouth until he forced her lips apart. Now all she could feel was the strength and warmth of his almost naked body. He wanted her and she could feel the tension growing in him as he held her. He reached for the clip at the back of her sun-top and then she felt his hand, hot against the soft swell of her breast. Instinctively she recoiled and put her hands up to push him away.

'No! Let me go! Damn you, let me go!'

Using all her strength, she broke free of his embrace, but his face darkened angrily and he reached for her again. She struggled wildly against him, doubling her fists and beating violently against his chest. He let her go so suddenly that she fell back into the shallows. For a moment they stared at each other, Sam's face wide-eyed and frightened, Mike's tight-lipped with scarcely controlled anger.

Harshly he said, 'You're my wife, Sam, I've every right in the world to kiss you like that.'

He stood glaring down at her, a big buccaneer of a man. No softness blurred his muscular figure, he was fit and hard. Sam realised with sickening clarity that he had only to exert his strength and she would be completely powerless, that he could force her to do anything he wanted. Strength and toughness, and the kind of sexuality that would completely dominate her if she ever gave it the opportunity. Pulling the sun-top up to cover herself, she slowly got to her feet, her eyes never leaving his face.

Tremblingly she said, 'Mike, please try to understand. Everything is strange to me, it's like being born fully grown. I've got to get used to the idea of being a person with no past. That—that takes some getting used to, believe me. And you—you say you're my husband. But to me you're a complete stranger, someone I met for the first time just a few days ago. I can't just pick up our relationship as it was before, because I don't know what it was like before. I don't know you and I don't know anything about you, except what you've told me and what I saw on the boat. I know that you're kind and brave and that you saved my life several times over,' he made an impatient gesture, but she persisted, 'and I'm more grateful for that than I can possibly say, but it isn't enough to make me want to ... to let you ...' She broke off in confusion and looked at him rather helplessly. 'Mike, I'm sorry, but I don't remember loving you.'

His jaw tightened and for a moment his eyes grew bleak. Then he put up a hand to push his wet hair off his face and turned to wade ashore. Slowly Sam followed him. He waited for her to catch him up and then said decisively, 'All right, Sam. I won't let things go so far again unless you want it as much as I do. But it's not going to be all on my side, you have to meet me half-way. You may not feel anything for me at the moment, but you've got to try and remember that I love you,' his voice roughened, 'very much. And try to think how you must have felt to marry me, will you?'

She gave a rather jerky little nod. 'All right, I'll try.'

'Good girl.' He continued to regard her for a moment and then stepped towards her. 'Here.' He picked up the straps of her sun-top and did the clip up for her. Despite herself, Sam began to tremble as his fingers touched her skin. 'Relax.' Deliberately he put a casual arm across her shoulders and led her back up the beach.

Sam tried to do as he asked, but that wild embrace in the sea had heightened her awareness of him and she found it well-nigh impossible to behave even naturally towards him, let alone meet him half-way as he wanted. Over the next few days she tried, Lord, how she tried, but every time he kissed her, however casually, she grew tense and when he tried to caress her she flinched away, and it was this physical rejection of him that angered Mike most of all. His face would become taut with suppressed emotion as he abruptly let her go, and he would turn to pour all his energy into the job in hand.

They walked round the coastline of the island until they found a break in the reef where a much larger stream, almost a small river, flowed into the sea, and here Mike built a shelter for them not too far from the shore. It was primitive as native huts went, with a roof and sides of interwoven palm fronds, but it protected them from the wind at night and from the sun by day. He even made one of the sides removable so that they could air the hut if they wanted to. Outside it he built another oven, a bigger one this time, so that whenever he caught a fish they could prepare it and leave it to cook slowly for their evening meal. Next he turned his attention to gathering all the dead wood

he could find into a bonfire a little way down the beach
and put lots of coconut fibre on it so that it could be
lit at once if ever they saw a boat or a plane. He had
fully recovered his strength very quickly and he put
all his energy into making their lives on the island
more comfortable, often labouring from dawn till dusk
and tiring himself out. Sam watched him, knowing
full well why he did it, and always with a feeling of
guilt at the back of her mind because she couldn't
give him what he wanted.

He kept his word in that he never let things get
out of hand, but he continued to kiss her often, although he did this less as the days passed and she still
failed to respond. Sam did try, but that episode on the
beach had given her a glimpse of the passion he was
capable of and she was afraid that any yielding on her
part would immediately fire it into burning life again.
Also she found the sensations he aroused in her whenever he kissed her vaguely disturbing. She felt no love
for him, and yet he aroused a feeling of sensuality that
heightened her senses and made her afraid of her own
reactions. Was it possible to want a man without loving him? She felt confused and unhappy. If only he
would leave her alone; she needed time to sort out her
own emotions. But he insisted on treating her with an
easy familiarity that bordered on possessiveness. It
was as if every time he touched her he was stressing the
fact that he had done it often before, that she was his
to take whenever he wanted. She realised that it must
anger him when she was careful not to let him see her
when she took off her clothes and bathed in the river,
especially when he must already have such an intimate
knowledge of her body, but she couldn't help it, she just

couldn't behave like a wife when she didn't feel like one.

When he finished the hut she had tried to make a bed for herself well away from his, but at this his face had grown dark with anger and he had dragged her across to his side of the hut.

'You're my wife, Sam,' he rasped out. 'We'll sleep together, even if it is only in the literal sense of the word!'

After that the tension had grown between them with every waking hour. Mike had carried on with his work, but there was a grim, set look on his face, and Sam had given up any pretence of trying to behave naturally towards him. Whenever he came near her, to show her how to prepare a fish or to open a coconut, she felt her heart start to pound and her pulses race. She supposed he was being very patient with her, and she could only guess at what such patience was doing to him. He was a man of dominant masculinity and her rejection of him must be like a physical blow every time. How long he could take it without losing control and forcing the issue she didn't dare to think, but she was terribly afraid that things must reach a climax soon, one way or the other. Her one hope was that a boat would come and take them off the island and back to civilisation, but even then the problem wouldn't be over, she would still be his wife; but at least they wouldn't be completely alone together for twenty-four hours a day with no respite from the electrically charged tension between them. She spent hours gazing hopefully out to sea in search of a boat and whenever Mike saw her his mouth grew grimmer and his manner more abrupt.

Late one evening he walked back to the hut from

the beach with some driftwood he had collected for the
fire they had lit. A full moon shed brilliance over the
island, an immense moon which turned from silver to
pale green and showered a pathway of diamonds over
the sea. He squatted down not far from her and the
firelight flickered across his face, softening his features.
A strange restlessness filled Sam and suddenly, without
apparent cause, the atmosphere between them was taut
as a bowstring.

She stood up abruptly. 'I'm going to wash in the
river.'

Picking up the blanket, she made her way a little
inland to where the river formed a small pool and
undressed in the shadow of a jacaranda tree. A thou-
sand scents hung in the night air and the island was
very still. Slowly she waded into the shallow river and
scooped up the water to wash herself. Moonlight
silvered her slim body, accentuating the shadows and
curves. Drops of water ran like quicksilver and she
languidly raised her arms to watch them run down to
her shoulders and on down her breasts. There was an
ethereal quality about the island tonight, the moonlight
giving it an air of enchantment and unreality. Almost
reluctantly, Sam stepped out of the water and, picking up the blanket, began to pat herself dry.

A twig cracked behind her and she spun round to
see Mike ducking under a branch as he came towards
the pool. He stopped dead when he saw her and Sam
pulled the blanket closer around herself, acutely aware
of the holes and rents in it. She felt her heart begin
to increase its beat and she said sharply, 'What do you
want?'

For a moment he didn't answer and then he said

evenly, 'You were a long time. I was afraid something had happened to you.'

'No, I'm all right.'

He began to walk slowly nearer and Sam immediately took fright.

'I'll be back in a minute,' she said quickly, hoping that he would go away.

But he kept on coming and she backed away until brought up short by the river.

'I've told you before,' he said. 'You don't have to cover yourself in front of me.' He reached out to pluck the blanket away, but she hugged it closer around her.

'No! Mike, please go away and leave me alone,' her voice rose in a panic.

His lip curled derisively and a contemptuous look came into his eyes. 'Grow up, Sam. You're a woman, not a twelve-year-old schoolgirl. Sooner or later you've got to face up to the fact that we're married. I've given you every opportunity to be natural, but you shy away every time I even touch you. How long do you need to get used to me, for God's sake—a year, two years?' His voice became more earnest. 'Can't you see that time isn't going to make any difference? Every hour that passes only puts us further apart. You say I'm like a stranger, but it's only because you're making me one, pushing me further and further away from you. And what's the point of continually looking for a boat? That's no way out. Even when one comes we still have to live together.'

He paused to see what effect his words had had on her, then he said roughly, 'I'm a man, Sam. I want you and I need you. I've been as patient with you as I know how, but I'm damned if I'll put up with this situation for much longer. You've *got* to come to terms with yourself!' When she still didn't answer, he said savagely, 'Don't force me to take you, Sam. I don't want to. Not that way. But you're leaving me with no choice.'

He looked at her searchingly, but her eyes were lowered and he couldn't read her expression.

'Oh, hell, what's the use in talking to you!' Abruptly he turned his back on her. 'Get dressed, I'll walk you back to the hut.'

But Sam didn't move. She stared at his broad back and almost for the first time she assimilated the fact that he was her husband, that he loved her and cherished her. What he had said was true; she was pushing him ever further away from her, making him even more of a stranger because she was afraid, afraid of giving herself to the closest relationship a woman can ever have with a man. But just because she had lost the memory of the love she felt for him it didn't give her the right to deny his love for her. She felt suddenly mean and selfish. And perhaps, if she let him do what he wanted, let him make love to her, then her feelings for him would develop into love. That he had the power to rouse her physically, she knew full well; surely something deeper might grow from that. And it would bring to an end all this unbearable tension and unhappiness between them.

She continued to stare at him, trying to find the courage within herself to take this, for her, gigantic step. She was so afraid, and yet there was no reason to be. Nothing was going to happen that hadn't happened before, she had just forgotten it, that was all. And then suddenly a thought came to her that gave her added strength: that perhaps—just perhaps—in his arms she might find the memory of that old love, so that for ever afterwards she could give herself to him in joy and thankfulness.

Very softly and chokingly she said, 'Mike.' He didn't hear her and she timidly reached out to put a hand on his bare shoulder.

It was the first time she had deliberately touched him, and the shock of it spread through his body like ripples on the river pool. His shoulder jerked and he swung round to face her, a guarded expression in his eyes. Still more than half afraid, Sam gazed into his tight face for a long moment and then bit her lip and looked away. Very slowly she lowered the blanket to her waist. She heard him take in his breath sharply and then say her name on a soft note of wonderment. He didn't attempt to come near her or touch her, he seemed to be waiting, and Sam instinctively knew for what. Her trembling fingers tightened convulsively on the blanket for a moment while she fought the need to cover herself again, and then she let it drop to the ground so that she stood naked before him. She began to shake with anticipation and fear.

Mike stood perfectly still for a long moment, letting his eyes drink their fill of her tall, slim body. All the emotions and passions which he'd been forced to hold back came surging to the surface and had grown and magnified a hundred times while under restraint. He longed for her, with a deep, yearning, wanting ache. When he took her in his arms she trembled violently but didn't try to draw away. He held her close to him, her head buried in his shoulder while he gently stroked her hair. He didn't say a word but turned her face to his

and kissed her on the mouth. It was the kiss given by
a man to the woman he loves, a kiss of fierce hunger
and growing passion. After only the briefest hesitation
Sam submitted, and her senses reeled under the im-
pact. Her eyes closed and she felt as if she was falling.
She gave a little moan and moved sensuously closer
to him.

Mike groaned, deep in his throat, and straightened
up. The moonlight lit his face, revealing the great light
of triumph in his eyes. He stooped for the blanket and
wrapped it round her, then picked her up and carried
her to the hut.

CHAPTER THREE

A CRY of pain and fear broke the peace of the night
and when he at last let her go, Sam lay in a tight ball
and wept convulsively. Mike reached out to comfort
her, but she fought him off.

'No! Leave me alone! Don't touch me!'

'Sam, sweetheart ...'

'Don't call me that! You liar! You rotten liar.' Great
sobs racked her body and she buried her face in her
hands.

'Sam, listen to me ...'

'No, I don't want to hear anything more from you.
You lied to me! You said we were married, but it wasn't
true. I'd never been with a man before—I was a virgin!
Did you think I was so stupid that I wouldn't realise?'
she cried bitterly as fresh sobs shook her.

'We *are* married, it was just ...'

'No, we're not. I don't believe you. You said we'd been married for over a week, what possible reason could there be for—for not consummating the marriage?'

'There *were* reasons.' He put his hand on her shoulder, but she shook it off angrily.

'What reasons? You're just telling more lies. I don't believe you,' she said again, her voice drowned in misery and humiliation. 'I've never felt as if I was married to you, and this proves it.'

Mike's voice hardened. 'All right, I'll tell you. We weren't able to choose the day we got married, we had to do it when we could. And I couldn't make love to you because—well, because it wasn't a convenient time of the month for you.'

'Oh!' Sam's face suffused with embarrassment in the darkness as she realised what he meant. Her crying stopped abruptly and she lay still for quite a long time, her back towards him. He didn't attempt to touch her, leaving her alone to recover, and presently she said in a painful whisper, 'Why didn't you tell me?'

Mike sighed and she felt him give a rueful shrug. 'If I had, you'd have been even more frightened of me. You seemed so afraid, and everything I tried to do only seemed to make things worse. If I'd warned you what to expect you'd have been so scared that you'd never have let me make love to you.'

Sam's voice was edged with bitterness. 'Not willingly, you mean.'

Mike's tone hardened. 'Not in any way, then. I've never yet forced myself on a woman, Sam, and I certainly didn't intend to start with an innocent girl.'

'Yet you threatened it,' she said stubbornly.

'Only to try and make you open your eyes, to face up to the fact that we're lovers, not just two strangers who happened to be cast away on an island together.' He turned on to his side to face her and stressed, '*Lovers*, Sam, in every sense of the word now, and that's how it's going to be—always.' He reached out and with his fingers traced along a shaft of moonlight that ran across her back and over her right hip.

Sam shuddered at his touch and began to cry again.

His fingers grew still and then Mike said harshly, 'Sam, don't cry, please don't cry. It cuts me up inside when you do.' And then he had turned her over into his arms and was kissing away the tears while Sam put her arms round his neck and clung to him in a torrent of weeping.

'Oh, sweetheart, I'm sorry. I know it's bad the first time, but it gets better, believe me. Trust me, my little love, trust me.' Her sobs eased as he went on kissing her, his lips hot against her eyes, her throat, her mouth, and ceased completely as his lips sought her breast and he whispered, 'Believe me, Sam, it gets better every time.'

And so he proved, using all his expertise and experience to awaken her body to the delights of sensuality and to light a fire within her that brought her again and again to the quivering heights of passion as the moonlight gradually gave way to the dawn. They slept then, their bodies entwined, but as the sun crept through the doorway, Mike tenderly kissed her awake and made love to her slowly, lazily, luxuriating in her youth and beauty as his eyes and hands explored her body. For a while Sam lay still, eyes closed, mouth slightly open, and her senses became throbbingly aware, then she opened her eyes and slowly reached out to touch him. He became quite still, but his breathing quickened as she lightly ran her fingers through the hairs on his chest and across the smooth, hard plain of his stomach. And suddenly his desire became urgent, almost frenzied, and gentleness vanished in a blaze of savagery as he took her and Sam's cry of ecstasy echoed through the clearing.

After that night the days became one long banquet of idyllic lovemaking and time passed them by without their noticing. On that first morning Sam had been shy and had turned her back on him to dress, but Mike had immediately put a stop to that and soon she behaved quite naturally in front of him. Not that she seemed to have her clothes on very often. Mike took great delight in her body; it was as if she was a piece of sculpture to be studied and coveted, to be felt with loving hands and experienced with mind and body. He would watch her appreciatively as she walked back along the beach after they'd had a swim, and then laugh at her because she averted her eyes and was too shy to look at him so openly. They lay in the sun and made love and slept and soon tanned a deep golden brown—all over. They had food and drink in plenty and a hut to protect them from the wind and the occasional fierce squalls of rain. And once they were on their way back from collecting mangoes from further inland when they were caught in an unexpected rainstorm. They sheltered under the spreading branches of a tree until it stopped as swiftly as it had begun and the hot sun made the jungle start to steam. The rain had brought the plants alive and the cloying,

sweet scent of the flowers and vegetation filled their
nostrils. There was an aphrodisiacal quality about it
that hung heavy in the still air. Mike turned Sam towards him and she saw in his eyes that he wanted her.
They lay together on the jungle floor and he passionately pulled her on top of him as raindrops fell from
the trees like liquid crystal and shattered on the parched
earth.

It was Sam who saw the boat first. She had been gathering wild bananas and was making her way back along
the beach to the hut, humming a tune and skipping a
little as she went. A movement on the water caught
her eye and when she looked up, she stood transfixed.
Then she dropped the bananas and began to run fast
along the beach, yelling for Mike at the top of her voice.
He came at the first sound of her shout and began to
run towards her, afraid that something was wrong,
but Sam gestured wildly out to sea and he turned to
look, coming to an abrupt halt as soon as he saw the
boat.
    Sam rushed up to him and grabbed his arm. 'Quick,
the bonfire!' she shouted excitedly, and began to pull
him back towards the camp.
    But he remained still while she jerked at his arm im-
patiently.
    'Come on, Mike. If we don't hurry it will be gone!'
    Then he swung round to face her and caught her
arm. He spoke with bewildering urgency. 'Let it go,
Sam. Why go back to civilisation when we're happy and
content as we are? We have everything we want here.
And we have each other. We can live as we like with
no one to invade our privacy. There couldn't be a more

perfect place for a honeymoon, even if we'd looked for months. Sam, we're happy here, let's keep it that way.'

She stared at him, her eyes wide with stunned surprise at the unexpectedness of his suggestion.

'But we can't stay here for ever!'

'No, not for ever, but there'll be other boats, we can wait for the next one, or the one after that.'

'We don't know that. There might not be another boat for months, for years!' The very thought of being stranded here for so long scared her. 'Mike, please, we can't take a chance like that. What if one of us gets ill? We *have* to light the bonfire.'

'Sam, if we signal that boat then the most wonderful part of our lives will be over, finished in just a few minutes. We'll be thrown back into so-called civilisation with all its stress and worries. Things won't ever be quite the same again. We'll have lost something very precious, something that we could hold on to for a little longer by letting that boat go.'

Her eyes were troubled as she looked up at him. 'You seem almost afraid to leave here. Is the world outside so terrible? I can't remember. I have no memories except of you and this island.' She looked at him searchingly. 'Is there something you're afraid of, Mike, something you haven't told me about?'

'No.' He answered too quickly and then tried to cover up by saying more gently, 'No, of course not. I just want to keep what we have now for a little longer, that's all. Isn't it worth trying to keep hold of, Sam? It is to me. Very much,' he added earnestly, his hand tightening on her arm.

Sam bit her lip and turned to look at the boat. It was closer now but was steering a course that would soon take it past the island. Slowly she said, 'Mike, if you let the boat go, then we'll have lost what we had anyway. It wouldn't be the same. I'd never be sure that you weren't trying to hide away from something you were afraid to face.' She looked at his suddenly set face. 'And I'm sorry, Mike, but I want to go back to civilisation. I want to see what the rest of the world is like. And all honeymoons have to come to an end some time, don't they? We can't make it last for ever.' She raised her eyes to his pleadingly. 'Please, Mike, light the bonfire.'

He gazed down at her for a second or two longer, a bleak look in his blue eyes. Then he said in a strange, cracked kind of voice, 'Oh, Sam, if you only knew what you were doing,' before he turned abruptly and went to take a red-hot brand from the fire and plunge it into the pile of coconut fibre and driftwood.

It lit at once and flamed into the sky with a column of smoke rising high above, luckily with little or no breeze to dispel it. Sam turned to gaze at the boat, shading her eyes from the glare of the setting sun. Surely someone must notice. They must, they must! But for what seemed ages nothing happened as she stared agonisingly across the sea, willing someone to see their beacon, and she began to be afraid that they'd delayed too long, that they were too late, as the boat continued on its course. She stood there with clenched fists, disappointment almost choking her, and she didn't dare look at Mike, standing silently behind her, because she knew that if she did she would let fly at him for having argued for so long and lost them their chance. Perhaps he had done so deliberately.

But even as she watched in growing despair, the

angle of the boat shifted and it started to come about. For a moment she was almost too afraid to believe her own eyes, but then her heart filled with elation as the boat definitely came round in a graceful turn and began to tack towards the island.

'They've seen us! Oh, Mike, they're coming!' She turned to him excitedly, but Mike was watching the boat with a grim, set look to his face.

'Go back into the jungle and stay out of sight until I call you.' She started to protest, but he silenced her as he said forcibly, 'We don't know who those men on the boat are, Sam. I want you out of the way until I know they can be trusted. Now, go on, move!'

There was no arguing with that tone of voice and Sam reluctantly went back to the hut and found her shoes, then stood just inside the screen of trees while she put them on and tried to tidy herself as best she could. The boat came nearer and she saw that it was quite large, an island schooner. It dropped anchor outside the reef and then two men lowered a dinghy over the side and climbed into it, pulling through the gap in the reef and rowing to where Mike stood waiting on the shore. The men got out of the boat and stood talking to Mike for some time while Sam peered anxiously out of the bushes. The man who appeared to be the leader was shaking his head firmly and seemed to be arguing. Surely he wouldn't refuse to take them? Mike frowned, but at length nodded, albeit reluctantly.

He walked back to the hut and beckoned her over. Quickly she ran to his side.

'The captain of the ship has agreed to take us off the island and give us a passage to St Vincent,' he said shortly.

'What was the argument about? Didn't they want to take us?'

'Oh, he was willing enough when we'd agreed a price, but it seems we're nearer Grenada and I wanted him to take us there, but he'd just come from the island and he absolutely refused to go back.'

'Does it matter so much—where we go?' Sam asked rather impatiently. 'Surely one place is as good as another.'

Mike looked at her for a moment and then turned away. 'Grenada would have been better for us,' he answered shortly. He went to pick up his knife from where he had been preparing a coconut that they would never now eat. 'Are you ready?'

'Yes.' His face looked so stern and withdrawn that she somehow felt guilty. Tentatively she put a hand on his arm. 'Mike, please don't be angry with me.'

He turned to look at her again and his face softened. Putting up his other hand, he covered hers, then gripped it tightly and pulled her roughly into his arms, kissing her with a fierce, bruising hunger that somehow seemed to have a touch of despair about it. When he at last took his lips from hers, Sam stared at him in astonishment, but he merely said brusquely, 'Come on, they're waiting. We'd better go,' and took her arm to lead her to the beach.

The hut had hidden them from view, but when they came into the open the men from the schooner both turned to look at her in surprise. The captain, a middle-aged, sharp-faced man, let his eyes run over her appraisingly and Sam instinctively moved nearer to Mike. His grip on her arm tightened reassuringly and he glared at the captain, who took one look at his belligerent expression and broad shoulders and hastily turned back to the boat. Mike helped her in and sat beside her while the other two men rowed them out to the schooner. There were two other members of the crew, both native Caribs, and they eyed her with open curiosity when she climbed abroad. They exchanged remarks in their own patois and laughed, but Mike made a biting comment in the same language and the sneering laughter was wiped from their faces. The captain gave the order to weigh anchor and soon they were sailing northwards, away from their island.

Mike came to stand beside her at the rail, his arm across her shoulders as they watched it slowly diminish into the distance. As Sam watched her eyes filled with tears. They had been so happy there, had led an almost idyllic existence after those first few days of tension before she had given herself to him. There they had reached glorious, dizzying heights of passion, and she had revelled in the new-found sensuality that Mike had taught her, so passionately, so lovingly. Everything there had been new and wonderful, and would never be quite the same again. A tear ran unbidden down her cheek and Mike gently used his thumb to wipe it away.

Softly he said, 'I'm glad you cried. I'm glad it meant that much to you.'

'Oh, Mike.' She buried her head in his shoulder and he held her close. Together they stood and watched until the island was nothing but a faint blur on the horizon, each full of the most poignant memories.

Later one of the crew showed them to a tiny cabin amidships where they were able to wash. He offered to lend Mike a razor to shave off the beard he'd grown, but Mike looked at himself in the cracked mirror fastened to the bulkhead and made a joke about it making him look more mature and said perhaps he'd keep it for a while longer. Sam hardly heard him, she went over to the mirror herself and slowly, self-consciously looked into it. On the island she had seen her reflection in the river, of course, but there it had always been broken and distorted and had given her no clear idea of her appearance. Now she stared at herself in pleased surprise as she examined each feature; her brows were finely arched over clear eyes that were mostly green with tawny brown specks and fringed with long, dark lashes. Her bone structure was good with high cheekbones, a slim, straight nose and a fairly determined chin. For several minutes Sam just stood and gazed at herself; no matter how much she had explored her features with her fingers, she had never imagined that she could look like that. Mike had said that she was lovely, but only now did she even begin to believe him.

She became aware that he was standing behind her, watching her, and her eyes met his in the mirror. Rather tremulously she smiled at him. 'I—I wish I had a hairbrush. I must look a mess.'

His face broke into a grin and he shook his head at her. 'Just like a woman! Ten minutes into civilisation and already she's worrying about what she looks like.'

And then Sam knew it was all right, that he'd forgiven her for not wanting to stay on the island. Happily she went to him and reached up to put her arms round his neck and kiss him.

'Why don't you shave? That beard tickles and I liked you better without it.'

'Because I wouldn't care to bet on how old that razor was or what it's been used for. I'd rather stay unshaven than run the risk of skin disease. Are you hungry? I'll go along to the galley and get us some food. Lock the door behind me and don't open it until I get back.'

'Aren't we going to eat with the crew?'

'No, best to keep to ourselves.'

'But why? Surely they wouldn't ...'

'Sam.' Mike caught hold of her chin and gave it a gentle shake. 'No one but these men know that we're even alive. I shan't be happy until we've landed safely at St Vincent. They're far too shifty for my liking.'

Sam looked at him in astonishment. 'But what possible reason can they have for wanting to harm us?'

Mike looked at her grimly. 'You just looked in the mirror, didn't you? If that didn't tell you why they might want me out of the way, nothing will.' Her eyes flew wide in sudden comprehension and he nodded. 'Just so. There are quite a few places on the South American coast where a beautiful white girl would fetch quite a high price. So you'll lock the door behind me and you don't open it again until you're sure it's me. Okay?'

Sam nodded and turned the key as soon as the door closed behind him, then stood waiting with beating heart until she heard a knock and then his voice telling her to open up.

The meal was some kind of stew washed down with a bottle of cheap wine and afterwards Mike made her lie down on the upper bunk and try to get some sleep.

'How long before we reach St Vincent?' she asked

him as she pulled the rather smelly blanket over herself.

'The wind is pretty strong, about noon tomorrow, I should think.'

He lay down on the bottom bunk, but Sam knew that he wasn't asleep. He had turned out the dim light, but the moon shone through the skylight, casting distorted shadows over the interior of the tiny cabin. Sam lay awake for a while wondering what tomorrow would bring, but presently she fell asleep, lulled by the gentle rocking of the boat.

It was a slight squeaking noise above her head that woke her and for a moment she was completely disorientated, not knowing where she was. Then the noise came again and she realised that someone was gently opening the skylight. She made a convulsive movement, but then Mike's hand came over her mouth and he breathed, 'Quiet, keep still,' in her ear. She obeyed him without question and lay with pulses racing, hardly daring to breathe, as the skylight opened further and a man's arm reached in holding a gun. Then suddenly there was a great shout of pain as Mike thrust the skylight shut again, trapping the man's arm and crushing it with the weight of the heavy skylight. The gun fell to the ground with a clatter and only after several minutes did Mike remove his weight from behind it and release the captured limb.

After that they were left alone for the rest of the night, although Mike still stayed awake, the gun now in his waistband, on the alert for some fresh attempt, and in the morning they stayed in the cabin until they saw land come into sight and they anchored in Kingstown harbour. Mike went to speak to the captain and then the dinghy was put over the side and the two Caribs rowed them to shore, but Sam noticed that the other crew man kept well out of the way while they were on deck and when she looked back she saw that he had his right arm in a makeshift sling. She shuddered, and a feeling of revulsion swept over her; as a first introduction to this new world it had been frightening in the extreme. If it hadn't been for Mike ... She turned to speak to him, but was surprised to see that he was directing the two Caribs to row them towards where a whole lot of similar boats were just coming in from a fishing trip and some way from the direct line to the shore. Soon they were swallowed up among the other boats, and when they landed on the shore Mike took care to keep among the people who had disembarked from them until they were well inland from the harbour.

Sam looked at him with a puzzled frown. 'Shouldn't we go and report to the authorities or something?'

'Plenty of time for that. We'd better find somewhere to stay first.'

He seemed to know his way about and led her into a side street behind the market. Sam had little time to look about her as he hurried her along the congested street, but she saw that it had a shabby appearance with old brick houses, high curbs and muddy gutters. The people who crowded the street were a mixture of races, with African and Carib being the most predominant, although there were also plenty of European faces amongst them. The crowds thinned out a little towards the end of the street and Mike led her to a seedy-looking doorway between two shops which had the word 'Hotel' in peeling letters over it.

Sam hung back, but he took her arm and led her firmly through the doorway. The hallway was dark

after the bright sunlight and it took a few seconds for
her eyes to adjust, but then she saw that there was a
small desk with a bell on it that Mike rang. After
a few minutes a very fat native woman came waddling
through a bead curtain at the end of the hall and
greeted them with a beaming smile.

Before she could speak, Mike spoke to her quickly
in the native patois and the woman threw up her hands
and exclaimed. Then she turned to Sam with her warm
smile and said, 'Don't you worry none, child, Big Annie
will take care of you and look after you as if you was
one of my own kin. Now you come along with me and
I'll show you to a real nice room.'

She led the way up two flights of stairs, puffing and
blowing, but talking all the time, and unlocked a door
at the back of the building. Sam found herself in a
largish room with a ceiling that sloped down at one
side to a long, low window. The shutters were closed
now against the sun, but when Sam pushed them open
she found that the room overlooked the left-hand side
of the harbour where there was still a lot of bustle
going on outside, but where it was relatively quiet after
the docks and fishing wharves. When she turned back
into the room she was pleased and surprised to find
that it was neat and clean, with a white-painted wardrobe and dressing table and a big double bed with an
ornate brass headrail. Sam flushed slightly at the sight
of the bed and then felt a flare of sexuality at the
thought of sharing it with Mike.

He was talking to Big Annie again, their heads close
together in earnest conversation and Sam turned back
to the window, drawn to the scene outside like a mag-
net. How she looked forward to exploring the town,

to becoming a part of that busy, noisy throng in the street below.

As soon as Big Annie left them alone she turned to Mike excitedly. 'Let's go out, shall we? I'm longing to explore. Do you know the town well? What are the best places to see?'

He looked at her indulgently. 'You're as excited as a kid on her first visit to town!' Then he frowned. 'But I suppose that's what it is for you since you lost your memory.' His face still serious, he sat on the edge of the bed and pulled her down beside him. 'Sam, Big Annie is fixing us some food and then I have to go out—alone.' He held up a hand to stop her protest and went on, 'All the money we have is what I had in my wallet when the *Venturer* went down. I have to arrange for some funds to be transferred here and also for new passports for us. Then there's the insurance company to be informed so that I can buy another boat. All that's going to take time and I'll be able to manage it much better alone.' He glanced ruefully down at his ragged and torn jeans. 'And I suppose the first priority will be some decent clothes.'

'But why can't I come with you? I can wait outside while you're seeing to all that.'

'No!' His voice was sharp and decisive. 'I want you to promise me that you'll stay in this room until I get back. I don't want you wandering the streets alone, do you understand, Sam?'

For a moment her lips pouted mutinously, but then Sam remembered the fright she'd got on the schooner and nodded. 'All right, I promise. But you will take me out to see the town later?'

'Yes, but I don't know how long I'll be.' He glanced

down at his wrist and gave a little sound of annoyance.
'Hell, I keep forgetting.'

'Forgetting what?' Sam saw a white band of skin on
his wrist and exclaimed, 'Your watch! What happened
to it?'

Mike gave a shrug. 'I gave it to the captain of the
schooner to pay for our passage. It was the price we
agreed.'

Sam was indignant. 'You paid him even though they
came after us with a gun?'

'If I hadn't he'd have told about finding us, and I
don't want to become an object of curiosity to the
whole island with our names in the newspaper and all
that rubbish.'

A knock came at the door and he got up to open it
for Big Annie who waddled in carrying a loaded tray.
The most delicious smells wafted to Sam's nostrils and
she realised that they hadn't eaten since the previous
evening. The native woman sat with them while they
ate, asking questions about the sinking of Mike's boat
and exclaiming with amazement at the loss of Sam's
memory, asking over and over again as if she simply
couldn't believe it, 'And you don't remember a thing?
Not nothing at all?'

When they'd finished eating she produced a shirt
for Mike to wear which was too small for his big
frame but would have to do for the time being, and
he left the two women alone.

'You seem to know Mike well?' Sam said curiously.

Big Annie nodded. 'I've known him for nearly two
years, I reckon. My eldest boy, Abe, he got in a heap
of trouble one time and Mike took him off the island
in his boat until everything died down and it was safe

for him to come back. I guess I'll always be grateful to him for that.' The older woman looked at her. 'He's a good friend to have, your man.'

She talked for a little longer and then brought up some crisp white towels and showed Sam where the bathroom was. The water heater was antiquated to say the least, but it gushed out gallons of lovely hot water and Sam lay back and luxuriated in it for ages, washing her hair and soaping herself with a tablet that smelt of lily of the valley, a long way from the Caribbean. The talcum powder had an entirely different scent, but she patted it on liberally anyway, thoroughly enjoying herself, and when she got back to their room she found that Mike had been back in her absence and left her a parcel containing a matching brush and comb. He must have also bought himself some new clothes because his jeans and the shirt he'd worn were lying over the back of a chair.

Opening the shutters again, Sam sat with her back to the window and let the sun dry her hair, using the hairbrush to flick up the ends, and then going to check the effect in the dressing-table mirror. It looked okay, but she didn't think she'd ever get used to this wide-eyed stranger who stared back at her from the mirror. She was wearing a bath towel wrapped round her sarong-fashion, and she let this fall to look at herself properly. Walking through the streets and seeing other women had shown her that she was tall, and now, as she turned in front of the mirror and squirmed to see her back view, she began to realise just why Mike took such delight in her body with its young, firm slenderness and softly rounded curves, the only flaw she could see was a small scar on the back of her left leg. The thought of Mike touching her made her flush and she hastily wrapped the towel round herself again and went back to the window to see if she could see him coming, but after an hour or so she began to feel tired and went to lie on the bed.

She was still fast asleep when Mike came back and he quietly slipped out of his outer clothes and lay down beside her. Sam subconsciously snuggled up to him and he gave a little grin as he smelt the soap and talc she'd used. His arm went protectively over her and then he, too, fell asleep.

When Sam awoke she realised with disappointment that it was nearly dark, but perhaps it still wasn't too late to go out. Sitting up, she disturbed Mike, who opened his eyes and looked at her.

'You smell like a flower garden,' he commented.

'Do you like it?'

'No, I prefer your natural smell.' He put his hand on the back of her neck and drew her down to kiss her.

'It doesn't seem to be putting you off,' Sam pointed out when she was at last able to raise her head.

He grinned. 'Nothing could put me off you. I'm hooked on you, woman, didn't you know?' And he tried to pull her down to kiss her again.

But Sam resisted. 'Mike, I'm hungry, and you said we could go out.'

'Mm, later.' He began to unwrap her towel.

Sam tried to keep it round her. 'No, Mike, you promised.' But his hands somehow got inside and she gave a gasp as he found her breasts. Feebly she tried to resist. 'No, not now, I ...' And then, as he began to caress her, 'Oh, Mike, love me ... love me ...' And it was a considerable time before she thought of anything but the need to be a part of him.

When they did finally dress and go out, Mike took her only a few yards along the street to a small restaurant where they sat in a shadowed alcove at the back of the room, which was so dimly lit that they could hardly see the faces of the other patrons, and were completely screened off when Mike let a curtain fall across the opening.

'It's the custom,' he said casually as he saw her disappointed look. 'And besides, I want to talk to you.'

A black waitress took their order and brought them glasses of sangaree to drink while they waited. Sam raised her eyebrows at the sight of the half-pint tumbler then sipped experimentally.

'It tastes good. What is it?'

'Sangaree? It's basically a wine glass of sherry or madeira topped up with soda-water with a little syrup and a teaspoonful of Cacao added.'

Although he'd said he wanted to talk to her, Mike seemed in no hurry to do so and it wasn't until they'd finished the meal of steamed flying fish followed by guava cheese and he was toying with the last of the drink in his glass that he began to tell her of his afternoon's activities.

'It will take a few days to transfer some money here, I'm afraid, and until then we'll have to go easy. Big Annie won't push us for payment, of course, but we'll have to save what cash we have for food and essentials.'

'Do essentials include some new clothes for me?' Sam asked hopefully.

'I think we can run to that,' he smiled. 'As long as you stick to something from the market.'

'Is that where you got yours?' she asked, looking

at the lightweight tan jacket and trousers he was wearing.

'Yes. The cut isn't exactly Savile Row, but they'll do for the time being.' He hesitated and then went on, 'It will take some time for the insurance claim for the *Venturer* to come through, so I've decided not to wait for it but to go ahead and buy another boat here.'

'Can you afford to do that?'

He nodded. 'It won't be custom-built, of course, and I shall probably only keep it until I can replace it with something I like better, but at least it will get us off this island.'

Sam looked at him in puzzlement. 'But I don't understand. Why do you want to leave here so soon? This looks like a lovely place. Couldn't we stay here for a while, Mike, please?'

He shook his head decisively. 'No, no longer than we have to.' Then more gently, 'I suppose I'm like all seamen, not happy unless they've got a deck under their feet. And I want to take you to England so that you can consult a specialist about your amnesia. Which brings me to the next thing I have to tell you. I went to enquire about replacing our passports, but although I was able to prove my identity from the things I had in my wallet, there was nothing, of course, to say who you were. I don't know where you were born, so we can't send for a copy of your birth certificate, and the certificate of our marriage went down with the *Venturer*, so rather than go to all the trouble and delay of sending to Barbados for a copy, I'm told it will be much simpler if we go through another marriage ceremony here. Then we can use that document to prove you exist and have you put on my passport.'

'Get married again?' Sam looked at him in astonishment.

'That's about it. I've arranged for the ceremony to take place in three days' time—that's the earliest you can do it, evidently.' He gave a mock frown. 'But it will be purely a formality, so don't get any ideas about having a white dress and flowers again.'

'Is that what we had last time? I wish I could remember it.'

His hand covered hers, warm and reassuring, and then he raised it to his lips and gently kissed her fingers. His eyes looked into hers and he said softly, 'I think it's time we went home to bed.'

Sam looked at him innocently. 'But I'm not tired.'

He grinned as he pushed back his chair and helped her to her feet. 'Nor am I.'

Any hopes Sam had of exploring St Vincent seemed always to be dashed; either Mike had heard of a boat he wanted to look at or he had a business appointment, and when he did take her to the market he made her put on a headscarf and a pair of sunglasses that he bought for her, telling her that all the women covered their heads. That the native women did seemed to be true, for they all wore straw hats or turbans under the huge baskets they carried on their heads, but Sam saw several European women, tourists mostly, without any head covering. But when she pointed this out to Mike he merely made a terse retort and told her to hurry up and choose what she wanted. He seemed in a great rush and hardly waited for her to choose an ethnic-print dress and a pair of sandals before hurrying her out of the market and back towards the hotel.

'But I need new underclothes,' Sam protested, and he reluctantly turned aside to find the right shop and waited impatiently while she picked out what she wanted.

Once back in their hotel room, Sam turned on him angrily. 'Mike, what is it? You make me feel like a criminal, hurrying me through the streets like that. And don't tell me it's because you're afraid I might be kidnapped or something, because I don't believe it. I saw several white women out by themselves today.'

Mike looked at her angry face and then put his hands on her shoulders. 'Okay, simmer down. It's just that I'm not exactly popular with the authorities here. I took Big Annie's son out from under their noses when they wanted to put him in prison, and although it was eventually proved that he hadn't committed the crime he'd been accused of, they weren't any too pleased with me and I was told in no uncertain terms never to show my face here again. That's why I didn't want to come here.'

'But why do *I* have to stay hidden away?'

'Because if you were spotted as a stranger and asked for your papers you wouldn't be able to produce any, and if I came forward to claim you they'd kick me off the island straight away—send me back to England probably, as I'm a British subject—and you they'd either put in custody until they could prove your identity or else send you back to Barbados.'

Sam stared at him in growing apprehension. 'They'd separate us?'

'I'm afraid so. Men in authority usually have long memories, you see, and they don't like people taking the law into their own hands. They'd hurt me if they could.'

'But what if you're recognised when you're in the town?' Sam's voice was sharp with fear.

'There's not much chance of that with this beard. And I know the town well, there's always somewhere to slip into if I think there's any danger.'

'But our passports? Surely the authorities must know you've applied to replace them?'

Shaking his head, Mike said, 'No, I've done everything through the British Consulate and they're discretion itself. And once we've been through the marriage ceremony and got a certificate we'll be quite safe, they can't possibly separate us then.'

But his explanation so frightened Sam that she lived in fear every time he went out and was reluctant to leave the hotel even to go to the nearby restaurant to eat. Even though no one paid them too much attention she was always immensely relieved when they got safely back to their room and she could only long for the three days to pass quickly so that at least half of their worries would disappear. She found that she was looking forward to the wedding ceremony; even though it was only a formality as Mike said, and there would be no bridal gown and flowers, she would at least have it to remember. She had a dress rehearsal when Mike was out looking at a boat, to try and take her mind off her anxiety for him, and felt far more feminine in the full-skirted dress. The sandals she had already tried on, but then she realised that she had forgotten to buy a handbag. She would have to ask Mike to get her one the next time he went out.

She waited, her fears increasing, until at last he came back and then she ran to hold him tight, overwhelmingly glad that he was still free.

'I've agreed to a deal on a boat,' he told her. 'It's an

oldish vessel, but she's seaworthy enough. I have to arrange for an expert to go over the engines, but once that's done and our money and passports come through we can leave here.'

They celebrated with a bottle of wine with their evening meal and afterwards, when they lay together in the big bed, their passion for the moment satiated, Sam said softly, 'Mike, tell me about our real wedding. Where was it?'

He was silent for a long moment, then he said, 'It was in an old stone church in the north of Barbados that was built by Jacobite prisoners who were transported there after the battle of Culloden. It's a lonely place, but it has a heartcatching view of the shore and the sea, and it's very small, only big enough for fifty people at the most. The day we were married the sun shone through the leaded windows and made patterns on the old, worn stones of the floor. It shone on the flowers I'd filled the place with, and it shone on you as you walked down the aisle alone when you came to me.' His voice grew husky. 'You looked lovely, so very lovely, in a simple white dress with flowers in your hair. You were afraid, and yet there was a certainty and radiance about you that shone out of your face, and put the feeble rays of the sun to shame.'

They both lay silently for a moment and then he picked up her left hand and began to play with her ringless fingers. 'I shall have to buy you another ring. I had to guess the size of the first one and it was too big for you; it must have come off when the boat went down.'

'Oh, Mike!' She moved into his arms and he held her tightly, his face buried in her hair. 'Oh, Mike, if

only the boat hadn't sunk. If only I could remember!'
And she stayed locked in the circle of his strength and
love, until she fell asleep.

The next morning Mike hurriedly did some shopping and brought the things back to the hotel and then
went out again to oversee the inspection of the engines
on the boat he'd chosen. Sam went down to join Big
Annie in her spotless kitchen and have a lesson in preparing a West Indian dish called pudding and souse
which was made from sweet potatoes and pumpkin
seasoned with herbs. It helped to take her mind off
her fear that Mike might be recognised, but at least
she had the comfort of knowing that in little more
than twenty-four hours now they would have the all-
important marriage certificate.

Towards noon Big Annie went out to buy fish from
the boats that had just pulled into the harbour, and
Sam went back upstairs to wait for Mike. She tried to
read a paperback novel that he'd bought her, but she
couldn't settle and wandered aimlessly round the room.
She sorted through the shopping he'd bought: new
socks and a tie for him, shampoo, lipstick, handker-
chiefs for her as well as a handbag. Picking up the bag
she held it against the sandals; it matched quite well
and she liked the style. It was stuffed with bunched-
up newspaper which she pulled out so that she could
put in her few possessions. That done, she went to
throw the newspaper away, but on impulse spread it
out and sat on the bed to read it. It was a copy of
the local daily newspaper, a very old one, dated over a
month ago, but it was still interesting to read of the
things that had made headlines then and were now probably completely forgotten. Idly she turned the sheet

over and then went suddenly tense as her eyes fell on
a large photograph in the centre of the page. It couldn't
be! It just couldn't!

Legs shaking, she slowly got to her feet and walked
over to the dressing table. Her pale face stared back at
her and then she looked at the photograph again. Yes,
there could be no mistake. It was definitely her own
image that smiled back at her from the news-sheet. For
a long while she gazed at this girl she couldn't remember and then, almost as if she were hypnotised,
she raised her eyes to the headline over the photograph:
'MILLIONAIRE'S DAUGHTER FEARED KID-
NAPPED'.

CHAPTER FOUR

FOR a moment the words danced in front of her eyes
and she felt as if she was going to faint, but somehow
Sam managed to pull herself together and to read the
caption under the photograph: 'Multi-millionaire
James Ashby, who owns considerable property and business interests in the West Indies and who has a branch
office in St Vincent, seen here with his daughter, Samantha, aged twenty-two, on board his luxury yacht
the *Medusa*.'

It took a little time for Sam to take this in, her brain
seemed to have become numbed by shock and it was
all too much to assimilate at once. She raised her eyes
to look at the man with the girl in the photograph.
He was in his late forties, she judged, but still an ex-

tremely handsome man, with only the slightest shading of grey at his temples. They were both dressed in clothes that were casual but obviously expensive and the yacht looked big and luxurious. And they both looked so happy, the man laughing and with his arm round the girl's shoulders. Could it really be her? Even now she couldn't really believe it. Almost she didn't want to believe it, because she had a sudden flare of jealousy for the girl who knew who she was and was secure in her father's love and her own environment. And if she and the girl were one and the same, what did it make her position now?

There was more about the story in the paper and Sam read it through carefully, but it didn't tell her a lot more. It mostly reiterated and enlarged on what had been in the caption, giving the address of the man's office in Kingstown and more details of his business interests, which seemed to range all over the world. It then went on to say that Miss Ashby had last been seen early one morning when she had left the family mansion in Barbados to go water-skiing. Her car had been found abandoned in the north of the island, but there was no clue to her whereabouts. No ransom note had yet been received, but it was feared that she had been taken away by boat and police throughout the West Indies were on the alert for any sign of her. It also said that Miss Ashby had often stayed in St Vincent and had many friends there.

Sam sat down on the bed and looked down dully at the paper. So that was why Mike had made her wear a headscarf and dark glasses when he took her to the market, why he'd made her stay in the hotel room all day and taken her to a cheap restaurant where she

wouldn't be recognised. And he hadn't really worried
about going out himself because it was only her they
were looking for, not him. But then why had he kept
the beard? Her numb brain wrestled with the problem
and all she could think of was that possibly he was
already a known criminal and was wanted for other
crimes. The enormity of the thought made her shudder
and for a while her mind shied away from the whole
thing, but as she sat there a great many things began
to fall into place: Mike's reluctance to talk about
himself and unwillingness to leave their island, her
lack of a wedding ring or any proof that they were
married, but, most of all, her overwhelming conviction
when they had first been shipwrecked that she wasn't
his wife and that she didn't love him.

She tried desperately to think back to when she had
regained consciousness in the boat; had he told her they
were married before he realised she had amnesia or
afterwards? It hit her with sickening clarity that it
was the latter, and she remembered how he'd hesitated
before he'd said it. Other things came back: his curt
denial that she had any family and the brusque way
he'd told her that nothing that happened before she'd
lost her memory was of any importance. Not of any importance! A father and possibly other members of a
family who were probably sick with worry about her.
She looked again at the newspaper item, eagerly read-
ing to see if she had overlooked mention of a mother
or brothers or sisters, but there was nothing. Still, even
to have a father would be a wonderful miracle.

There was the sound of footsteps coming up the stairs
and, afraid that it might be Mike, she hastily folded
the newspaper and hid it at the back of the drawer

where she'd put her underclothes, but the footsteps went on by and she could breathe again, released from the suffocating fear that had suddenly filled her. Fear? Fear of Mike? But he had never hurt her physically in any way. Even when he had wanted her so desperately he hadn't forced himself on her, had let her make the first move. No, but he had threatened violence and there was no knowing how much longer he would have held himself in check. Doubt raged through her mind. Could he possibly have been speaking the truth? She might have run away to marry him, against her father's wishes, after all she appeared to be rich and he was just ... just what? A drifter, one of those people who just sailed eternally to different places and never settled anywhere, a sea-tramp?

And if he'd kidnapped her why did he want to marry her? So that he could suck more blood-money out of her father to keep it quiet? But he'd saved her life. Of course he had, she wasn't worth any money to him dead. The arguments raged back and forth in her brain until she had an agonising headache, but still she couldn't leave it alone. In the end it all boiled down to the fact that Mike had said he loved her. If that was a lie, a pretence to make her give herself to him willingly ... Oh, God, she had to know the truth, she just had to, or she would go mad! She sat with her head in her hands, her thoughts an agonising turmoil.

When Mike came back she was sitting waiting for him, outwardly calm. He looked tired, but he had a smile and a hug for her before he went to shower and change.

'After we've eaten perhaps you'd like to go for a walk

in the Botanic Garden near Government House,' he suggested as he put on a clean shirt.

'In the dark?'

'The scents of the flowers come out then; and you could do with some exercise, you look pale.' He crossed to her and bent to kiss her lightly on the forehead. 'I'm sorry, Sam, I know it hasn't been any fun for you these last few days, but I'll make it up to you, I swear it.'

An overwhelming urge to throw herself into his arms and tell him all about the newspaper article was countermanded by a feeling of revulsion because his professed concern might only be a sham, so she just sat still and did nothing, her hands clasped tightly together in her lap.

She managed to say with just the right edge of worry, 'What if we're seen?'

'There won't be much moon tonight and if we see anyone we'll just have to go into a huddle and pretend to be a courting couple. Not that that will be any hardship,' he added with his crooked grin.

But for the life of her Sam couldn't respond and she merely turned away to pick up her bag.

They went to the usual restaurant, but she couldn't eat and Mike looked at her in concern. 'What's the matter? Aren't you well?'

'I—I have a headache. Tell me how you got on today,' she added hurriedly, afraid that he might guess.

'Everything's going along fine. The engines need only minor adjustments and the owner's agreed to do that straight away, and the Consul tells me that my money will be through tomorrow and that if I take the marriage certificate along to him immediately he'll be able to give us our passport, so we shall be able to leave

St Vincent tomorrow night on the evening tide.'

Tomorrow? Sam gazed at him in alarm; she hadn't realised that everything was happening so quickly. A surge of panic filled her. Tomorrow they would be married, whether they had gone through a ceremony before or not, and then they would leave here and be alone together again on the high seas where he couldn't be traced, where there would be no one to come to her rescue. She had to know the truth before then, somehow she had to make him prove himself tonight.

With nails digging cruelly into her palms beneath the table, she said, 'Mike, don't I have any family at all who would like to see me married, who would come to the ceremony tomorrow?' and gazed at him searchingly, eager for any reaction.

His eyelids flickered, but he didn't look at her. 'Is that what's worrying you? No, I told you there's no one.'

Sam had to bite her lip hard, but she forced herself to go on—after all, he might not have known she had a father. 'Back on our island, you said that we had to get married when we could, that we couldn't choose the time. Why was that?'

He looked at her then, his blue eyes trying to read hers, and Sam quickly looked down at her plate.

'It just worked out like that. There was no point in waiting.'

'I wasn't—we weren't running away from anything or anyone? You'd tell me if we were?'

There was a short silence and then he said harshly, 'No.' He caught her chin and turned her face round to look at him. 'Why are you asking all these questions now? You're not—you're not starting to remember things, are you?'

Sam looked at him, sure now that he was lying, a hard ball of grief and disillusionment growing inside her. 'Why, don't you want me to remember?'

His eyes regarded her steadily and his reply shook her. 'I want it more than anything else in the world. I always have.'

She dropped her eyes and said dully, 'No, I'm not starting to remember. I just wondered, that was all.'

They left the restaurant and began to thread their way through the outskirts of the town. Sam had never felt less like wandering through a tropical garden, but she was afraid of arousing his suspicions further, and even more afraid of being alone with him in the hotel room and having to lie beside him in the big bed. They walked around the gardens for the better part of an hour, and it was as he'd said, the flower scents stole unforgettably into the air and clung to the night until she could hardly bear it. There were a few other people about, mostly young couples, so that thankfully they didn't have to pretend to be lovers. Pretend? A few hours ago it would have been true, but not now, not any more.

When they got back to the hotel she undressed quickly while Mike was in the bathroom and was already lying huddled in bed when he came in. Silently he undressed and put out the light and climbed in beside her. Sam moved as far away as possible, but he reached out for her and tried to pull her to him.

'No!' she said sharply. 'I told you I have a headache.'

He chuckled. 'Only married a few weeks and already you're having headaches?'

'I mean it, I'm not pretending.'

'So I'll try to soothe it away.'

He put his arm round her and began to stroke her forehead gently, but after only a moment Sam could stand his hypocrisy no longer and jerked angrily away.

'Damn you, leave me alone, can't you?'

His voice was terse as he moved away. 'All right, I've got the message. I'm sorry. I hope your head feels better in the morning,' and he turned on to his side.

Sam lay miserably in the darkness. She wanted to cry out her hurt and humiliation but was afraid to in case he heard her and forced the truth out of her. What she was going to do about the situation seemed of little importance, all that mattered was that Mike had lied to her from the start. Everything, right from the beginning, had been one big lie. It was obvious now that she wasn't married to him and he had only said so to stop her trying to find out who she was. And it had kept her at his side when they were rescued, made her believe him and obey him when he'd spun her the tale about being wanted by the police. Wretchedly she wondered why he'd kidnapped her. Simply for money, she supposed, with the threat of selling her to a brothel on the South American coast if her father didn't pay up? Running into that storm must have really upset his plans. He must have had it all worked out, and her loss of memory must have been a godsend after they were shipwrecked.

Suddenly terrible pictures began to come into her mind. She remembered a phrase he'd used on the boat, something about 'do I have to knock you unconscious again?' Then he had been joking, but now it made her wonder if he had in fact knocked her out when his boat was sinking. Had she struggled with him, tried to get off on her own? And if she hadn't lost her memory, what would he have done to her then if a boat had rescued them? Would he have terrified her into keeping quiet?

She trembled violently and Mike stirred, so that afterwards she lay very still, hoping he would think that she was asleep. Memories came back to her then, pictures of what really *had* been. Mike giving her their last drop of water, of his hands, raw and bleeding after rowing for hours on end, of his holding her when they hit the reef, and of his half carrying her to look for water on the island when he was already so weak he could hardly stand. He'd said he wouldn't let anything happen to her and he'd kept his word, but he had also said that he loved her, and that could only have been a lie.

Sam had thought that by giving herself to him it would reawaken a love she'd forgotten. It hadn't, there had been no sudden awareness of love, only an aroused passion and a fulfilled physical need that had quickly grown into something deeper. He had the power to arouse her sexually and to make her give herself to him time and time again and to glory in the giving, but she still didn't know if that was love. She had thought that everything would be clear cut; you either loved someone or you didn't, but all thoughts of analysing her feelings had been lost beneath the tide of passion and physical delight that had consumed her.

Her fingers dug into the pillow in helpless anger and wretchedness. Oh, why have you done this to me, Mike, why? Her thoughts became bitter. Mike Scott—she didn't even know if it was his real name!

By the time morning came, Sam had made up her mind what she was going to do. She lay in bed while Mike dressed, but then he came over and gently shook her.

'Hey, sleepyhead, wake up! We've got a busy day ahead of us.'

Sam sat up in bed and pulled the sheet up; they'd never got round to buying any nightclothes. She found that she couldn't look Mike in the eye, so instead leaned back against the bed rail and closed her eyes again.

Mike looked at her white face and dark shadowed eyes in concern and came to sit on the edge of the bed. 'Headache still there?' She nodded slightly and he put his hand on her forehead. 'You feel a bit hot.' The anxiety in his voice increased. 'Are you sure you'll be all right to go through with the wedding this afternoon?'

Sam gripped the bedclothes tightly and tried to keep her voice steady. 'Yes, I'll be all right.'

'Good girl. You'd better stay in bed and rest this morning. I'll get Big Annie to bring you up some breakfast and a couple of aspirins. Unfortunately I have to go out to make sure the boat is properly provisioned before we leave and also to buy you another ring. Here, give me your finger and let me measure it.' He made a loop in a piece of string and knotted it round her finger. 'That should do it. Is there anything else you want me to get you while I'm out?'

'No.' She shook her head, still not looking at him.

'I'll be back as soon as I can, but it may not be for a few hours, but don't worry—I'll be here in plenty of time for the wedding.' He bent to kiss her, but Sam hastily turned her head away. He looked at her for a moment and then said quietly, 'Isn't it rather late to have wedding day nerves, Sam?'

'It—it isn't that.'

'Then I must have upset you in some way. Won't you tell me what it is?'

'No, there's nothing.' Her voice was little more than a whisper.

'So why won't you kiss me goodbye?'

Somehow she made herself look at him and found him watching her with a quizzical expression in his eyes. Leaning forward, she went to give him a light kiss, but the moment her lips touched his she was lost and her arms went round his neck and she pressed her mouth against his fiercely as if she'd never let him go. When she finally did, she leaned her head against his shoulder and said huskily, 'Goodbye, Mike.'

He looked at her in wry amusement as he put her from him. 'I got more than I bargained for then, didn't I?' He stood up and looked down at her. 'Rest now, sweetheart, I'll see you soon.'

When he'd gone Sam lay back against the knobbly bedhead, eyes tight closed, her hands gripping the covers, willing herself not to cry. Crying wasn't going to help now. There would be time enough for that later. Presently Big Annie came in carrying a break-fast tray of coffee and toast with the promised aspirins and sat with her while she ate it, exclaiming in sympathy at her headache. She was being kind, Sam knew, but she wished with all her heart that the native woman would go away so that she could get what she planned to do over and done with.

At last she waddled away, saying that she had to get to the market, and Sam hardly waited for her footsteps to recede down the stairs before she jumped out of bed and dressed herself in her denims and sun-top. After making sure that there was no one about, she ran lightly down the stairs and into the street. The doors of the restaurant were open and a woman was sweeping out the place. Sam slipped past her and into the public phone booth in the small foyer. With trembling hands she picked up the receiver and nerved herself to speak to the operator.

'Please, I'd like to place a person-to-person call with Mr James Ashby of Ashby Incorporates in Barbados. I'm sorry, I don't know the number, and could you please reverse the charges.' The operator asked who was calling and she had to gulp twice before she could get it out. 'Would you tell him it's about Miss Ashby?'

Sam waited for what seemed an eternity, the operator occasionally coming back over the crackling line to tell her that she was still trying to place the call. The phone booth was set back against the wall, but Sam still huddled into it, afraid that Big Annie or Mike might walk by and see her.

The male voice, when it did come, almost startled her out of her wits. 'Who is this?' it demanded harshly. For a few minutes Sam was too shaken to speak and the man, angry now, said, 'Hello, who's there?'

'H-hello. Is that—is that Mr Ashby?'

'No, this is his secretary. Who is this? Do you have some news of Miss Ashby?'

She ought to have guessed that she wouldn't be put straight through to such an important man; he had probably had dozens of crank phone calls. Her voice gathered more strength as she replied, 'Yes, I think I know where she is.'

'Where?' The question was snapped out.

'I want to speak to Mr Ashby personally.'

'He's a very busy man.' Then, rather cuttingly, 'Don't worry, you'll get the reward if your information leads to his daughter. You can tell me.'

Sam mentally squared her shoulders. 'No, thank you. If Mr Ashby wants to find his daughter he'll have to talk to me himself.'

There was a short silence and then the voice said, 'Wait!'

Which she did, for nearly ten minutes of growing anxiety, before another man's voice came on the line, more modulated, much more polite.

'Good morning, I believe you have some information about my daughter's whereabouts?'

Huskily Sam said, 'Yes.' Was this her father's voice? She didn't know, it brought back no memories.

'If you have, I shall be very grateful, and you will, of course, be well rewarded. Perhaps you could start by telling me where you saw her?' The tone was gentle, persuasive.

Sam's voice, however, was cracked and unnatural as she said, 'Does your daughter have a scar on—on her left leg?'

There was a sudden silence and then James Ashby said tersely, 'Yes. Yes, she does. Do you know where she is?' he demanded sharply.

'Yes, I think so. I think I'm your daughter.'

This time she heard him gasp before he said, 'Is this some kind of a sick joke?'

Sam gave a sobbing laugh. 'Yes, I suppose you could call it that.'

'Samantha? Samantha, is that really you?' The voice was fierce, urgent.

'I—I don't know. I'm not sure. I saw a picture of

you with your daughter in the paper and it looked like me and I have a scar on my left leg. So I think I am, but I don't know, I just don't know any more.' Sam's voice became incoherent as she finished speaking.

'What are you talking about? Who are you? How can you possibly not be sure?' James Ashby demanded angrily.

Sam bit her knuckles and tried to pull herself together. 'I was in an accident and I lost my memory.'

Now it was his turn to sound almost incoherent. 'You —you mean you can't remember anything, not even who you are?'

'No, nothing. He—he told me that I was his wife and I believed him, but—but yesterday I saw the picture in the paper.'

'Who? Who told you that you were his wife?'

In little more than a whisper, she answered, 'He said his name was Mike Scott.'

And now, incredibly, he believed her. 'Samantha!' He gasped out her name. 'Oh, Samantha, my dear child.' There was another silence while he recovered himself and then he said urgently, 'Where are you?'

'I'm in St Vincent. We're staying at a hotel in Kingstown in a street that runs between the waterfront and the market. I—I don't know the name of the street and the hotel doesn't seem to have a name, but it's owned by a woman called Big Annie.'

'Where is Scott now?' His tone had become completely practical.

'He went out. He's bought a boat and we're going to leave tonight.'

'I see. Are you in the hotel now?'

'No, I'm in a restaurant just along the street. It's called the Fontabelle.'

'Do you know your way round the town?'

'No, he made me stay in the hotel room.'

There was a muttered imprecation and then James Ashby said, 'How long will he be away?'

'Several hours, he said.'

'Then I want you to go back to your hotel room and wait for me there. Don't worry about me not finding the place, I have people tracking it down already. What's your room number?'

'Number six, on the second floor.'

'All right. Now, I have a jet plane standing by at the airport. I'll be with you very shortly.'

'What—what if he comes back?'

'Then I want you to try and keep him at the hotel as long as you can. If he tries to take you away, then make an excuse to go to the bathroom and lock yourself in and don't come out. Can you manage that?'

'Yes, I suppose so.'

'Good. Now try not to worry. I'll be there as soon as it's humanly possible. I'm going to ring off now so that I can get started. See you soon, Samantha.'

See you soon; they were the very words that Mike had used when he said goodbye to her. She wondered with a sick feeling of fear which one of them she would see first. Slowly she replaced the receiver. Suddenly shock set in and she leaned back against the grubby graffiti-covered wall of the phone booth and began to shake. What if she'd done the wrong thing? What if she really was Mike's wife? What if she had made a mistake and she wasn't Samantha Ashby? Panic ran through her in waves; she couldn't go back to their room and just wait, just sit there until someone walked through the door and directed her life one way or the other. Blindly she stumbled out of the restaurant and into the street, to be immediately caught up in the throng of people and carried along. Everyone seemed cheerful and laughing as they called out to one another. Sam gazed at them in resentful bewilderment, jealous of their happiness when she was being dragged unwillingly through this hell that circumstances had forced on her.

She found herself in the market and wandered aimlessly in between the lanes of goods. How long did it take to fly from Barbados to St Vincent? How long before James Ashby arrived? She supposed she should have asked him. In her mind she thought of him only as James Ashby. She gave a gulp of almost hysterical laughter; how could you think of a voice on the telephone as your father? For a long time she wandered unseeingly up and down the market, her mind torn by doubts and fears, a fierce, darting pain shooting through her head. A clock on a distant church tower told her that it was past midday; she ought to go back, one of them would be coming for her soon, soon. Again panic flowed, but then a thought came that she caught and held on to tightly; if James Ashby could prove to her that he was her father then she would be sure of her identity and sure of her relationship with him, she would at least have one truth to cling to out of the welter of lies and uncertainties. And right now that was all she wanted, all she could hope for.

Coming out of the market she found that she was lost at first, but then saw some old houses that she remembered Mike had pointed out because they were built of bricks brought as ballast in the holds of sugar schooners and she knew where she was. Quickly now, afraid in case anyone got there before her, Sam made her way back to the hotel. It looked all right, there was no car or anything outside. But she couldn't relax until she had reached their room and found it empty. Thank goodness, Mike hadn't come back. She collapsed on the bed, out of breath, but after a few moments sat up and took some more of the aspirins that Big Annie had left for her. God, how her head ached! It felt as if saws were being dragged through her brain.

It was impossible to try to relax, she jumped up every time she heard the slightest noise, her nerves on edge. The time wore on and she began to be afraid that Mike would come back first. He would wonder if he found her dressed like this instead of ready for the wedding, so she went into the bathroom to wash and then changed into the dress and sandals, combing her hair with an unsteady hand and not even attempting the lipstick.

From below she heard the sounds of footsteps coming rapidly up the stairs and she turned to face the door, her eyes wide and dark with tension. There was a sharp rap on the door. So it wasn't Mike. She went to go to the door to open it but found she couldn't move. The knock came again, louder, impatient. She managed a hoarse, 'C-come in.'

The door opened and a man stood on the threshold. It was the man in the photograph, only this time he was conservatively dressed in a well-cut light-grey business suit. And he wasn't smiling, his face was creased with an anxious frown. But the moment he saw her the frown was replaced by a look of triumph and he began to rush across the room towards her.

'Samantha!'

Sam backed away from his outstretched arms. 'Who are you?'

He stopped abruptly and stared at her, then pulled himself together. 'I'm sorry—I hadn't realised. I'm James Ashby, I'm your father, my dear,' he said earnestly.

'You—you think I'm your daughter, then?'

'Darling, I *know* you're my daughter.'

Sam bit her lip. 'Could—could you prove it to me, please?'

His eyes widened incredulously, but then he reached for his wallet and said, 'Of course.' He took some papers out and handed them to her. 'Here's my driver's licence with a photograph on it, that will prove to you who I am, and yes, here's a copy of the poster I had printed offering a reward for finding you.'

Sam looked at the poster. It was a much better photograph, taken in close-up so that she had no difficulty in recognising each feature of her own face. The reward was for a quarter of a million Barbadian dollars or its equivalent in any currency. So that was another reason why Mike had kept her hidden away. Slowly she folded it and gave the things back to him.

'Yes, it would—it would seem that I am your daughter.'

Suddenly her legs wouldn't hold her and she sank on to the bed, burying her face in her hands. James Ashby sat down beside her and put his arms round her, holding her head against his shoulder.

'Oh, my poor child! But you're safe now, safe from that swine who took you away from me.'

For a few seconds Sam nearly succumbed to the

temptation to cry out her relief on his shoulder, but the mention of Mike made her sit up with a jerk.

'We must go! He might come back and find you here. He might try to keep me with him.' She stood up agitatedly and tried to pull him to his feet.

'No, it's all right, there's no need to be afraid of him any longer.'

'But you don't know him. He's terribly strong, he could knock you down. Oh, please!' She began to tug at his sleeve, to make him move towards the door.

'Samantha, listen to me.' Her father caught her by the shoulders in a firm grip. 'I tell you it's quite safe. Look if you don't believe me.'

He let go of her and opened the door. Sam looked past him and saw two hefty men waiting outside in the corridor.

'Who are they?' she asked in little more than a whisper.

'They are in my employ, and I have another man waiting downstairs in the street. So you see there's really nothing to be afraid of any more. I don't think any man could knock down all four of us, do you?' he added with a slightly twisted smile. He drew her back into the room and made her sit down. 'Now, before we leave I want you to tell me everything that happened to you. How did you come to lose your memory?'

'I—that is, he told me I hit my head when his boat sank.' Falteringly at first, but then with growing confidence she gave him the bare outlines of their time in the dinghy and on the island, finishing with their arrival at St Vincent. 'Then I saw the photograph in the paper. Look, here it is.' She went to the drawer and got the news-sheet to show him, explaining how she found it.

James Ashby read it through quickly and then looked at her. He seemed about to say something, hesitated, but then said grimly, 'On the phone you said that Scott had told you you were his wife and you believed him.' His eyes went pointedly to the bed. 'This set-up—does that mean that you—that he made you—live with him as his wife?'

Sam flushed painfully. 'Yes.' And then, at the look that passed over his face, she added almost angrily, 'Of course he did. What the hell did you expect? That I'd spent weeks alone with the man and still be—and still be ...' She broke off and put her head in her hands, shaking uncontrollably.

Immediately her father got to his feet and put his arms round her, holding her close. He swore violently. 'That swine! I'll kill him for what he's done to you! But first I'll make sure that he lives to regret it, I'll make him beg to die!'

'No!' Sam pulled away from him and stared at him appalled. His eyes, his face, were twisted by hatred. 'No, please, you mustn't. You don't understand.' She sought for the words to convince him. 'Apart—apart from that he was always very kind to me, he looked after me. And he never hurt me. In fact he saved my life more than once.'

'You call taking you away from your home, from me, and fooling you into letting him do what he wanted to you, you call that being kind?' he asked, his voice savage.

Sam's voice rose. 'I could have died! When we were in the boat we only had a little water. He could have kept it all for himself, but he shared it with me—no, he gave me more than my fair share—while he went without himself.' She gazed at James Ashby, her face white and set. She said clearly, 'If you want me to come back with you then you must give me your word that you will do nothing to harm Mike. You won't tell the police where he is or do anything in—in revenge for kidnapping me. You won't try to hurt him in any way. I mean it,' she added as she looked at his suddenly grim face. 'If you don't give me your solemn promise then I won't go back with you.'

His chin came out and for a moment she thought he was going to refuse, but then he gave a resigned shrug. 'All right, Samantha, if that's what you want. And maybe it's better that way; at least there won't be any more publicity and you'll be able to put all this behind you and forget it.'

Sam gave a sigh of relief. 'Thank you. Thank you,' she hesitated, then added tentatively, 'Daddy.'

James Ashby looked at her, a strange light in his eyes, then he put his arm round her shoulders and kissed her gently on the forehead. 'Let's go, the sooner I get you home the better.'

Hopefully Sam said, 'Will there be anyone waiting? Do I have a mother, brothers and sisters?'

His mouth gave a kind of jerk. 'No, baby. I'm sorry, you only have me.'

He led her down the stairs, the two men going ahead. At the curb there waited a big American car, a convertible with the hood down. James Ashby opened the door for her, but just as she moved forward to get in she heard a shout behind her. 'Sam!' Turning round, she looked down the street and then stood as though turned to stone. Mike was only about twenty yards away! He began to run fast towards them, dropping the parcel he was carrying and dodging between the pedestrians.

Sam was too paralysed to move, but her father picked her up and bundled her into the car anyhow, jumping in after her.

'Get going!' he yelled to one of his men who had already got into the driving seat.

Another man turned to grapple with Mike. He was built like a heavyweight boxer, but Mike brushed him out of the way like an annoying fly. But it had given the driver the necessary few seconds he needed to start the engine and start to pull away. Mike leapt forward and grabbed the side of the car. He caught hold of Sam and began to lift her bodily out of it. Her father hung on to her so that she felt as if she was being torn in half. Mike's strength began to tell, but then the third man ran round and put his arm round Mike's throat, trying to force him off. Mike had to release one arm to throw the man off and her father pulled away from him as the car gathered speed, blaring a path through the crowded street. Sam had one last look into Mike's agonised eyes as he called her name and then he had fallen off the car, rolling over and over in the dusty road.

CHAPTER FIVE

FOR a long time Sam was too numb to take any notice of where she was being taken; her mind was haunted by that look in Mike's eyes. No matter how long she lived she would never forget the look of anguish when he'd had to let go of the car. She sat in the back seat, oblivious of James Ashby's attempts to comfort her and blind to her surroundings even when they reached the airport and she was helped aboard a small executive jet plane that immediately took off for the return trip to

Barbados. Looking down, she saw St Vincent gradually becoming smaller beneath the wings. A green island, with hills reaching the sea, the volcano, Soufrière, still active and a source of menace and constant danger. Sam thought of Mike still down there on the fast disappearing island and felt a sudden cold fear, but whether it was fear for him or of him she was too confused to tell.

They flew on over the Atlantic and her father eventually left her side and went to a sort of communications console set into the plane where he proceeded to have a conversation over the radio. Sam didn't take too much notice of him, but she felt a sort of release from anxiety now that it was over and she had someone to take care of her, someone whom she knew she could trust and who had her best interests at heart.

When they landed at Seawell Airport and the plane taxied to the far side of the airport away from the main complex, she turned to him in some trepidation.

'I don't have a passport. It was lost when Mike's boat went down and then he—he arranged for me to be put on his new passport as his wife.'

'It's all right, you don't have to worry about that, or anything else. I radioed ahead and everything's been arranged.'

And it had, most efficiently. The plane went straight into a hangar that seemed very dark after the bright sunlight and there was a luxurious car waiting for them as soon as the plane rolled to a stop. Her father took her arm and helped her down the steps, spoke a brief word to a man in a uniform with lots of gold braid and then ushered her into the air-conditioned interior of the car. Sam noticed that it also had darkened windows so that no one would be able to see in. She began to realise how money could be used to make wheels run so smoothly; James Ashby had just whisked her out of St Vincent without a passport or any form of identification, whereas it had taken Mike nearly four days to try to achieve the same object.

They drove inland from the airport before picking up the main highway leading into Bridgetown. Sam looked out at the town, glad of something to take her mind off unpleasant memories. The streets were busier even than Kingstown, but there was an air of greater affluence with lots more cars and seemingly hundreds of people on bicycles, many of whom looked curiously at the big, chauffeur-driven car as it picked its way surely through the streets. She realised that she had been completely silent for some time and tried to think of something to say.

'Is it always as crowded as this?' she managed.

James Ashby turned to her quickly, glad that she seemed to have got over her numbness.

'Yes, always; this is one of the most highly populated islands for its size in the West Indies. Look, we're just going through Trafalgar Square and there's Nelson's Column, much smaller than the one in London, of course.'

He pointed out other places to her: public buildings, a cathedral, Government House; soon Sam became bewildered by all the names and sights but did her best to look attentive because it seemed to please her father. Several times he asked her whether she didn't recognise a place, but she always had to regretfully shake her head. At last they left the town behind and took a road he told her was called Highway One and that ran northwards parallel to the coast past the popular Paradise Beach resort that was crowded with people and on past more long, tree-shaded beaches of soft sand and into the stretch of coastline known as the Gold Coast where large hotels lay hidden behind trees and opulent homes beyond palm-fringed drives.

Soon they turned into one of these driveways between high iron gates which opened electronically when the chauffeur pressed a gadget in the car. The house was nearly a quarter of a mile from the entrance and set in beautifully landscaped gardens of immaculately manicured lawns, with trees and shrubs exactly positioned to give a false look of naturalness to the surroundings. The house looked fairly new from its design and this, too, although built of coral stone, had a regimented look about it with its precise Palladian architecture.

But Sam hardly had time to take any of this in before her father hurried her inside and up a wide staircase. Other people fell in behind them and James Ashby started to give orders over his shoulder. There was something about issuing a statement for the press, withdrawing the reward offer, increasing security, the sharp commands went completely over her head. At the top of the staircase he led her to the left and through double doors into a sitting-room furnished with priceless antiques and with a bedroom opening off it. There were three people waiting for them in the sitting-room; a thin, middle-aged, but very prosperous-looking man, a sharp-faced woman in a well-cut but simple dark dress in her late thirties, and another woman in nurse's uniform.

Her father said, 'Samantha, this is Dr Langdon who already knows the details of your amnesia and who is going to give you a physical check-up. And this is Mrs Gregory, my housekeeper. You already knew them both very well before you lost your memory.' He didn't bother to introduce the nurse. Turning her round to face him, he put his hands on her shoulders and smiled at her encouragingly. 'Now, I want you to go with the doctor and let him make sure you aren't suffering from anything. That diet you lived on when you were ship-wrecked couldn't have been good for you. I'm going to leave you now to deal with the work your return has involved, but I'll come and see you just as soon as Dr Langdon is through. All right?'

Sam nodded rather reluctantly; she would have much rather gone somewhere to be alone with him, to talk and ask him about the part of her life she couldn't remember. There was so much she wanted to know. But he had said he would come back, so there would be time then.

After he had gone the nurse led her into a large and very luxurious bathroom with a sunken marble bath that opened off the bedroom. Here a maid was waiting and the two women helped her to undress. Sam pro-tested that she could manage, but they looked at her in astonishment and insisted on helping her, not letting her do a thing, until Sam began to feel like a doll—that or someone who was so imbecilic they couldn't help themselves, she thought wryly.

Once she was bathed and back in the bedroom, wear-ing only a very thick towelling bath-robe, the doctor made her sit down while he examined her throat and the rest of her head, the nurse standing beside him to hand him the instruments he needed and the housekeeper—what was her name?—Mrs Gregory, that was it, hovering in the background.

The doctor felt her head very carefully. 'Did you feel a lump on any part of your head after you were hit?' he asked her.

'No, not a lump, but I had a cut here.' She lifted her hand to touch her right temple. 'I had to have a dressing on it.'

'Ah, yes.' He probed delicately. 'No sign of it now. Does it hurt you when I touch it?'

Sam shook her head but added, 'At first it hurt terribly, but now I only get headaches when I try to concentrate very hard or when—or when something happens to worry me.' Her voice slowed and she looked away.

'Hm.' He straightened up and said, 'I'm afraid I don't have any experience of amnesia, but I've already recommended a specialist to your father and I believe he's contacting him now and arranging for him to fly out here, so we should know what the chances of your recovering your memory will be within the next few days, with any luck. But at least I can make sure you're not suffering from anything else. Take off your robe and lie on the bed, would you?'

Moving to obey him, Sam began to take off the robe, but became aware of being watched and looked up quickly to find Mrs Gregory's eyes fixed on her. The eyes were cold and hard in the sharp face and Sam gave an involuntary shiver, but as soon as the housekeeper realised Sam was looking at her, her mouth lifted into a smile that didn't reach her eyes and she moved solicitously forward.

'Let me help you, my dear.'

But Sam shrugged off the robe and lay down on the bed, acutely aware of the woman's eyes running over her slim body, her face a strange mixture of expressions but which to Sam seemed very much like hate and jealousy.

The doctor's stethoscope was cold on her chest as he prodded her and asked her how long she had been without food and water in the dinghy, and what food she'd eaten on the island. He made her turn over on her front for a while, but when she turned back his examination became far more intimate and brought a flush to her cheeks.

Afterwards he removed the plastic glove he had been wearing and said, 'There doesn't seem to be much wrong with you apart from the amnesia, but you've been through a great deal of stress lately and I think a couple of days of bed rest with nourishing food and a course of vitamins to make up for the deficiency caused by lack of protein should help a great deal. Perhaps if you have complete quiet it might relieve the headaches too.' He looked at her keenly. 'You have one now, don't you?'

Sam nodded and confessed, 'I've had it for two days.'

'Why didn't you tell me? I'll get you something to relieve it at once.' He looked at one or two packets in his medical bag but gave a dissatisfied shake of his head. 'No, I don't think these are suitable for you. I have some others in my office that will be better. I'll go and get them and be back directly.'

'Oh, please, you don't have to go to all that bother. A couple of aspirins will do.'

Dr Langdon gave her a rather strange look but insisted on getting the special pills. He left the room with Mrs Gregory and the nurse helped her into a long, delicately tucked Victorian nightdress that felt blissfully soft to her skin and then pulled back the covers of the bed. The sheets were of silk and the bed so soft that it provided a vivid contrast to the other places she had slept lately: the wooden floor of the dinghy, the piled leaves in the island hut, and the rather lumpy mattress on the bed in Big Annie's hotel. For a moment despair gripped her and she felt a sudden surge of loneliness and grief. Oh, Mike! Mike! But she bit her lip determinedly; she had made the choice, hadn't she? She had chosen what she knew to be the truth instead of lies and deceit. All right, so those weeks on the island had been glorious, but it had been nothing but sexual passion, she didn't love Mike and he only pretended to love her. Making a fool of her every time he took her.

It was quite a long time before her father came up to see her, but Sam turned to him eagerly. He sat on a chair beside her bed and took her hand.

'How do you feel?'

'Fine. Please, there's so much I want to ask you. About my mother, and about you. I want to know everything, the things we did together, why we live here.'

She would have gone on, but he held up his hand. 'Of course you do. But don't let's rush things—there's plenty of time. I've got a specialist flying out from Switzerland immediately and I think we should wait on his advice before I go into too much detail. It might not be good for you to hear everything at once.'

'You have someone coming out from Switzerland?' Sam said in surprise.

'He's the best in the world,' James Ashby said with

a touch of pride. 'Of course he didn't want to come straight away, said he had a clinic full of patients, but I told him to name his price and of course that made him change his mind fast. It always does,' he added cynically.

Sam looked at his lips, twisted in contempt, and for the first time began to wonder about her father as a person. But she had little time before he turned to her and said intently, 'But one thing I am sure of, and that's that you must put all thoughts of the last few weeks you spent with your kidnapper out of your mind completely. You must pick up your life just as if nothing had happened, try to look on it as just a bad dream that's best forgotten.' His voice became sharper. 'And there must be nothing left to remind you of Mike Scott, do you understand me, Samantha?'

Sam looked at his tense face with a puzzled frown. 'I suppose so. But how can I pick up the threads of my old life if I don't remember what they were?'

Immediately his face relaxed and he gave what to Sam looked like a rather relieved smile, although she couldn't think why. 'You'll find that easy enough, but we'll wait until the specialist has examined you before we make any plans.' He stood up. 'I believe Dr Langdon's back with your pills. And don't forget, there's nothing to worry about,' he emphasised as he left.

Soon afterwards the doctor came back with the nurse and gave Sam two bottles of vitamins to last for a couple of weeks. Then he handed her two large white tablets to take. He hesitated before giving her a glass of water to swallow them down and said, 'Your father did talk to you?'

Sam nodded, thinking he meant about the specialist,

and he gave her the glass. She swallowed them down, hoping that they would help her headache which was now really bad. But evidently those pills weren't for the headache after all because he produced another bottle from which he took one capsule.

'This should help your head. But only take one a day, they're quite strong.'

'I shall rattle if I take all these pills,' Sam managed with a weak smile.

'Well, we won't start the vitamins until tomorrow. Now, Nurse Taylor here will stay with you all the time, night and day, while you're in bed, and you must tell her if you feel at all unwell. Do you understand?'

'Why, yes, but I'm sure it won't be necessary.' Sam couldn't understand why he and her father looked at her so intently.

He went away and the nurse went to sit quietly in an armchair by the window and read a book. Presently Sam slept, waking in the late evening feeling dopey and not at all refreshed. The nurse gave her a glass of hot milk, but she'd hardly finished it before she fell asleep again.

The stomach pains began in the early hours of the following morning and at first she was in such a deep sleep that she merely tossed and turned uncomfortably, but then a fiercer pain gripped her and she woke up in a sweat. For a moment she couldn't think where she was and she called out in a panic, 'Mike!' Instantly the nurse was by her side and she seemed to know immediately what was the matter. She gave Sam a drink that was a help and a hot water bottle to put on her stomach. And presently she helped Sam to the bathroom and then found her what she needed. The pains weren't so bad now, but she felt completely drained, her hair damp with perspiration.

When Sam was tucked up in bed again, weak and listless, she lay for a little while with a feeling of relief. Was that all it was? For a while she had been afraid she was going to be really ill. She wondered if it hurt like this every time. But she had no way of knowing, it hadn't happened to her since she had lost her memory. Suddenly her thoughts stopped short; she began to do sums in her head. There had been the week in the dinghy, and another week before she and Mike had made love, then the rest of the weeks on the island. She came to an abrupt stop and then feverishly counted again. Could she possibly have been ... Oh God, no! Her mind shied away from the possibility.

Then suddenly a lot of things fell into place: the way her father and the doctor had looked at her, and her father saying so earnestly, 'And there must be nothing left to remind you of Mike Scott. Do you understand?' But she hadn't understood, she hadn't understood at all. How could anyone who'd lost their memory understand a thing like that? And how could her father—her own father—have let the doctor go ahead and give her the pills? Surely he must realise that she wasn't the type of person to—but perhaps he thought that she *was* that type of person. Someone who could casually destroy anything that might have unpleasant associations. But she wasn't—she wasn't like that at all. And now it was too late, too late! Sam turned her face into the pillow and silently began to weep.

She seemed to sleep most of the time the next day, only waking to eat and feeling muzzy-headed the whole time, until at last she realised that she must have been given a heavy tranquilliser. After that she refused to take the 'headache' pill the nurse offered her; better to have a splitting head than to sleep all the time. For a few hours she still felt disorientated and she dozed fitfully, but gradually she became more aware of her surroundings and could think coherently again. At first she felt an overwhelming sense of bitterness against her father for permitting such a thing to be done to her, but slowly fairness and reason came back and she realised that from her father's viewpoint he had been ridding her of something that could have completely ruined her life, been a constant reminder of what he thought must have been a terrible time for her. He wasn't to know that that part of it had been quite the reverse, it was the lies that had been used to bring it about that had been terrible. And he had thought that she understood and was in agreement with his wishes.

So gradually the bitterness faded away and resignation came; there was nothing she could do about it now, better to try and forget and to do as her father said and try to pick up the pieces of her life again. But somehow she knew that she would never be able to accept what had been done to her, she would only learn to live with it.

The doctor came the next day and with him the specialist from Switzerland. He was an austere little man with a grey moustache and inclined to be rather taciturn until Sam gravely apologised for taking him away from his other patients. He looked at her for a long moment and then his brow cleared and his eyes twinkled at her.

'Let me see what I can do for you, *ma fille*,' he said in his broken English.

He felt her head and gave her lots of tests, most of which didn't make any sense at all to Sam. He questioned her closely about her headaches and told her to make her mind a blank and then to delve down into the far reaches of her mind to try to remember anything, anything at all. Sam tried, she tried harder for him than she'd ever done before, until she gave a whimper of pain from the great searing bands of hurt that tore through her head. He stopped immediately and Sam was thankful to lie down on her bed, her nerves palpitating and wet with perspiration. Dr Langdon wanted her to have another of his tranquillisers, but she refused to have anything but aspirin and the specialist backed her up on this.

'It is most important that she should not rely on drugs to relieve the pain. She must learn to try to avoid any situation that would bring on a headache.'

For the rest of the day she stayed quietly in her room, but towards evening her father came to sit with her. She looked at him steadily as he sat down and he flushed a little and looked discomfited. Sam had the sudden disquieting feeling that he had known she hadn't understood what he meant the other evening but had gone ahead anyway. Quickly she pushed it to the back of her mind; she just couldn't stand any more lies and deceit.

He cleared his throat and said abruptly, 'I've been talking to the Swiss doctor. The news isn't very hopeful, I'm afraid. He seems to think that if your memory was going to come back it would have done so by now, either the whole or in part. He did say that a great shock or another blow on the head might bring it back quite suddenly, but the chances of that happening are, of course, quite remote.'

Sam looked down at the coverlet and picked at the edge. 'I see.'

Her father's voice became encouraging. 'But that isn't so bad. In no time at all you'll be completely caught up in your old life again. I thought that the best thing would be to invite your closest friends here one at a time. We'll tell them what's happened, of course, so that they don't try to rush you into accepting return invitations to parties and that sort of thing. But to take it slowly at first, I think. What do you say?'

'Yes, I suppose so,' Sam answered dully.

'If you don't feel up to meeting anyone yet you only have to say. We'll do just whatever you want,' James Ashby said with an anxious note in his voice.

Sam realised that she was being miserable and tried to smile. 'That seems fine, honestly.'

He gave an over-large smile in return. 'Good, then I'll arrange for someone to call in a couple of days. Perhaps we'll start with Paul.'

'Paul?'

'Yes, he was one of your closest friends.'

'All right, if you say so.'

He went to move away but Sam put out a hand to stop him. 'Daddy, please won't you tell me about my mother?'

He became very still for a moment and then he said abruptly, 'Your mother is dead.'

'When did she die?'

'A long time ago. You were only a child. You wouldn't have remembered her anyway,' he added caustically.

Sam could see that it was painful for him to talk about it, so she changed the subject and asked him about himself instead. He was immediately more loquacious and spent quite a long time telling her about his youth in England and the lucky business deal that had formed the basis of his empire at a very early age. He spoke proudly of his possessions, the flat in Mayfair in England, the new house on the coast in Miama, Florida, his yacht, the list seemed endless. 'But I prefer to make my base here,' he finished, 'it's a closer-knit community and people here understand what success really means.'

He went away after that as he had a dinner appointment and Sam was left to eat a solitary, but beautifully prepared meal, alone in her room. In the morning the nurse didn't want her to get up, at least until Dr Langdon had been, but Sam just couldn't stand lying in bed any longer, she needed fresh air and sunlight, so she overrode all protests and determinedly got out of bed. There was a dressing-room opening off her bedroom and when she pushed aside the doors of the wardrobes that lined the walls she just stood and stared. They were bursting with clothes! Skirts, blouses, slacks, tops, swimsuits—and dresses! every kind of dress from long evening dresses through day dresses to tennis dresses. A great profusion of materials and colours that made her feel giddy.

'Do you mean to tell me these are all mine?' she gasped.

The maid gave a prim nod. 'Oh, yes, Miss Ashby. And there are other things in here.' She opened another cupboard to reveal drawers full of gorgeous silk and lace underwear and yet another with racks and racks of shoes, nearly all of them frivolous-looking and with very high heels.

'Good heavens! I haven't the faintest idea what to choose. What do you think? I'm sorry I don't remember your name,' she apologised.

'It's Preston, Miss Ashby.'

'Preston?' Sam's brow wrinkled. 'But I'm sure I don't call you that. Don't I call you by your first name?'

The woman spoke decisively. 'No, Miss Ashby, your father wouldn't like that.'

Sam could find nothing to say in answer to that, so she turned back to the Aladdin's cave of clothes and chose a dress at random. Then she sat at the huge, ornate dressing table to select some make-up from the dozens of bottles and tubes she found in the drawers there. When she'd finished experimenting she sat back and looked at herself critically. Suddenly the previous occasion when she'd tried on new clothes and looked at herself in the mirror came flooding back; then she had been happily trying on the cheap dress that Mike had bought her in Kingstown market for her wedding. Closing her eyes, she let the memory of that happiness steal over her, only to recall with bitterness how later she had picked up the handbag and seen the photograph.

But nevertheless she turned to the maid and said, 'The dress I was wearing when I arrived here the other night, where is it?'

'Oh, that,' Preston sniffed disdainfully. 'I took it down to the incinerator and burnt it at once.'

'I see.' Sam turned away and blinked hard. They were certainly doing their best to destroy every reminder of Mike.

She spent the rest of the morning sitting in a lounger on the patio at the back of the house, but at lunch time her father came home and they ate together. This must have been quite a rare occurrence from the way everybody flapped around and Sam got little enjoyment from the meal with servants in the room all the time, but afterwards he asked if she felt up to being shown round the house. Sam agreed eagerly, looking forward to hearing stories of their life together, but it turned merely into a conducted tour, her father talking like a museum guide as he pointed out each rare antique ornament or piece of furniture, telling her where he had acquired it, how much it had cost at the time and was worth now, and usually who he had beaten down to get it. It was obvious that he was passionately fond of all the pieces, his face lighting up as he talked of them, but Sam, who had asked questions at first, gradually found herself becoming more and more quiet. She couldn't help but wonder whether his love of the pieces was a genuine love of the beautiful workmanship or just the love of possessions.

Eventually noticing her silence, he turned to her with an exclamation of self-reproach. 'I'm sorry, Samantha, I got so carried away in showing you round that I forgot you must be getting tired.'

Sam gave a small smile. 'I think I would like to rest, if you don't mind.'

'Of course not.' He pressed a button set into the wall. 'I'll tell Mrs Gregory to take you upstairs. Have a good rest today and I'll show you the other part of the house tomorrow.'

'Oh, that won't be necessary,' Sam said hastily. 'I can manage alone.' And when the housekeeper came she refused her help and climbed the lovely staircase that her father told her had been brought from an Italian palace. Behind her she heard him saying something to Mrs Gregory about moving one of the ornaments and when she reached the landing and looked back they were in animated conversation, the woman's face more alive than Sam had ever seen it.

A short sleep revived her completely and as night fell she became restless again. There was a television, a radio, and a music centre with masses of records and tapes in her sitting-room, but after watching the television for a while she became bored and decided to go downstairs and find her father. She supposed she should have called the maid, but instead Sam picked out a pretty dress in shades of turquoise with long full sleeves and a circular skirt. She added matching sandals and fresh make-up and then, satisfied with her appearance, she left her room and went down the corridor to the landing.

It was a long landing, stretching the width of the house and part of it was in shadow. As Sam walked along it she heard a commotion which seemed to be coming from outside. Her father must have heard it too, because he came out of a room that she now knew to be his study and angrily called for the butler.

'What's all that row? Go and see what's happening.'

The butler hastily ran to the front doors and opened one side, but before he could say anything he was roughly pushed aside and the other door flung backwards on its hinges to crash against the wall. Three men erupted into the hall. Or at least one came in, the other two were trying to drag him out, but the first man did a tricky sort of turn and banged the other two's heads together so hard that they staggered away and slumped to the floor. Then the man turned and Sam saw Mike face her father.

'I've come for my wife,' he said grimly.

CHAPTER SIX

FOR a moment there was dead silence as the two men faced each other, her father in his white tuxedo over-shadowed by Mike, who looked entirely different in a well-cut suit of some dark material that somehow managed to make him appear taller and broader. And he was clean-shaven again, his jawline strong and firm.

Her father, his voice furious, said, 'How the hell did *you* get in here?'

Mike gave a slight shrug and straightened his tie. 'I climbed over the wall.'

'You couldn't have, the top of the wall is electrified.'

'Not now it isn't.' Mike's mouth twisted into a grim smile.

James Ashby glared at him. 'If you don't get out of here at once I'll call the police and have you arrested for breaking and entering.'

'Go ahead,' Mike said coolly. 'Some rather interesting facts might come to light if you do.'

Her father's fists clenched and he became even more furious. He turned to another man who had followed him from the study. 'Stevens, don't stand there like a fool, go and round up the rest of the men.'

The man turned and ran towards the back of the

house, but Mike seemed in no way perturbed, he even smiled a little. 'It won't do you any good, Ashby. I'm not leaving here without Sam. Where is she?'

He glanced upwards and Sam automatically drew further back into the shadows.

Mike moved towards the foot of the stairs, but her father barred his way. 'You keep away from my daughter, Scott. She's suffered enough at your hands.'

'Oh, really?' Mike's voice was suddenly scathing. 'And just what do you think she went through in yours? Get out of my way, Ashby. I want my wife.'

He went to push her father aside, but the older man grappled with him, shouting to the butler to help him. One of the men who had been stunned joined in, but even so Mike would have pushed them aside easily if two other men hadn't run in then through the front door, and one of them carried a heavy blackjack. He lifted this to bring it down on Mike's head, but he saw it coming and jerked his head aside. But even so the glancing blow it gave him was enough to stun him for a moment and the men were able to overpower him and hold him while James Ashby stared at him in triumph.

'I told you to get out, but you wouldn't listen, would you? You're going to be very, very sorry for that.' And suddenly he hit Mike hard in the stomach. Then he stood back. 'Take him outside and deal with him. Make sure he learns never to come here again. And I'm not too worried about his face being so smashed up that no other woman will ever look at him again either,' he added cruelly.

Mike began to struggle, but the men now held him so firmly that his efforts were completely futile and they began to drag him towards the door.

Life and movement suddenly came back into Sam's stunned body and she shouted, 'No! No, stop!' and began to run towards the stairs.

Immediately every face turned to look up at her. Her father gave an exclamation of surprise and annoyance and moved to bar her way while Mike began to struggle even harder. At the foot of the stairs Sam turned angrily on her father.

'You promised not to hurt him. Is this the way you keep your promises?'

'Samantha, you don't understand. He broke in here to try and kidnap you again!'

'Kidnap? How can you kidnap your own wife?' Mike demanded, but his voice was immediately choked off as one of the men put his arm round his throat.

Her face white, Sam faced her father defiantly. 'Are you going to keep your promise or not?'

James Ashby glared at her and then shrugged. 'Oh, very well. I'll just have him thrown out, but he must give an undertaking that he won't come here again. I refuse to be threatened in my own home.'

He looked towards Mike, but Mike's lips curled disdainfully. 'If you think you're going to get any promises out of me, you're crazy. I want Sam back and I'm going to get her!'

'You see!' her father said explosively. 'There's no reasoning with a man like that. It will be much better to teach him a lesson he won't forget now, so that we'll be finished with him for ever.'

'No, there must be some other way.' Sam drew him aside. 'Let me talk to him, explain that I don't want to go back to him.'

'No. He'll try and turn you against me. Tell you a lot of lies to make you believe in him again. I'm not prepared to take that risk.

'There isn't any risk because I won't fall for anything he tells me, not after the way he lied before. And when he realises I mean it, he'll just go away and there won't be any more trouble.'

'No, Samantha, it's a chance I'm not prepared to take,' he said firmly. 'He might turn nasty and hurt you. He's capable enough of it,' he added, rubbing the side of his jaw where a blow from Mike's fist had caught him.

'No, he won't. He's never hurt me. Please, Daddy. Let me try it my way,' Sam begged, reaching out to touch his sleeve.

He looked at her for a long moment and then sighed. 'All right, but just for a short time—and I'll be right outside the door if you need help.' He turned to address the men holding Mike. 'Let him go,' he ordered.

Slowly they did so and Mike shrugged himself back into his jacket which had been almost torn off in the struggle.

James Ashby glared across at him. 'My daughter has persuaded me to let her talk to you. But just remember that we overpowered you once and we can do it again, so don't even dare to think of lifting a finger against her.'

Mike looked at him balefully. 'I'm not the one who's harmed her.'

Sam looked at them both in distress and said, 'Oh, please,' on a note of pleading.

Immediately her father opened the door of a small library and said, 'You can go in here.'

Sam went in and Mike followed her, shutting the door firmly behind him. For a moment they just stood and stared at each other, but then Mike opened his arms and said, 'Oh, Sam, sweetheart, what have they done to you?'

It was obvious that he expected her to run to him, but Sam turned away and said coldly, 'Why did you come here, Mike? You must have known that the place was guarded.

He became very still and then he slowly lowered his arms. 'I came to get you back.'

'Why?' Sam's voice was sharp with bitterness. 'So that you could still collect my ransom money? And to go through another wedding so that you could push the price up even higher, is that it?'

Mike took two paces across the room and caught hold of her upper arms. 'What the hell are you saying?' he demanded fiercely.

Sam's tone was icy. 'Take your hands off me.' Slowly he did so and she went on, 'You know perfectly well what I mean. I've seen your lies for what they are. I know that you kidnapped me and took me away ...'

'That isn't true,' Mike broke in urgently. 'I knew your father would spin you a whole lot of lies once he found out you'd lost your memory. Things couldn't have worked out better from his point of view.'

'You do admit that he's my father, then? Even though when we were together you denied that I had any family—more than once.'

'Only because you'd sworn that you wanted nothing more to do with him, that as far as you were concerned you had no family any more.'

'Deny my own father? You expect me to believe that?' Sam said incredulously.

'I know it's difficult and I know he must have told you lots of lies about me, but believe me, Sam, I only did it for your sake. And you must leave here with me now, tonight. I don't know how he found you and took you away from me last time, but I'll make darn sure it doesn't happen again. This time we'll take a plane and fly ...'

Sam interrupted him coldly. 'He didn't find me. I saw an article about me in a newspaper and phoned him to ask him to come for me.'

Mike flinched as if he'd received an even harder blow in the stomach. 'You did that, without giving me the chance to explain? And after everything that had been between us, everything we'd meant to each other?' he added unbelievingly.

'I did give you a chance to tell the truth, on our last night together. I asked you if you were sure that I hadn't any family and you said no, definitely. And as for—for the rest, you just used me. Used me as a sex-object. Laughing when you tricked me out of my virginity and laughing every time you fooled me into ...'

'Sam, that isn't so!' He caught her by the shoulders and gripped her hard, his fingers digging into her flesh. 'I loved you. I always loved you. You're the most wonderful thing that ever happened to me. And I'm not going to let that lying hypocrite separate us. Sam, can't you remember anything that happened before?'

'No, nothing. Mike, let me go, you're hurting me!'

But his grip on her shoulders tightened and he began to shake her, so overwhelming was his need to get her memory back. 'Sam, you've got to remember, you've got to!' he said fiercely.

'No! No, I can't. Oh, please, Mike, don't! Mike, stop it!' Her voice rose in fear as her head began to pound.

Suddenly the door burst open and then Mike was being dragged off her, but she didn't see what happened to him because the room started to sway and rock around her in the most peculiar manner and she fell in a dead faint on her father's prize Persian carpet.

When Sam came to she found that she had been carried up to her room, the nurse again in attendance, and she didn't see her father again until the next day when he came up to see how she was. She asked him then what had happened to Mike, but all she could get out of him was that he had been thrown out, so she had no way of knowing whether or not he had kept his promise.

He did, however, keep his word about letting her friends start to visit her, because the following day, as she was sitting on the terrace eating a rather belated breakfast of Bajan musk melon, he phoned to say that he was bringing Paul home to lunch. Sam remembered that he'd mentioned the name before and supposed that Paul must be the son of a neighbour, someone of her own age. So it came as rather a shock when her father ushered in, not a youth, but an extremely handsome and self-possessed Frenchman of about thirty years old.

He immediately crossed the room to where she was standing and took both her hands in his. 'Chérie!' Lowering his head, he kissed her hands and then moved to kiss her on the cheek, but drew back before he did so. 'Ah, but no, I must not. I must try and remember that I am again a stranger to you. We must start again from the beginning and I must stifle all the words that are in my heart and which I long to say to you.'

Sam looked at him in bewilderment, completely taken aback, he was so different from what she had expected.

Her father came smilingly to put a hand on the Frenchman's shoulder. 'I've told you that you must be patient, Paul. Samantha has been through a terrible ordeal. Samantha, my dear, this is Paul de Lacey, *Comte* de Lacey,' he emphasised. 'You and he were—very good friends.'

'Oh. Do you—do you live in Barbados, Monsieur de Lacey?' Sam didn't quite know what to say to the handsome man before her.

'But yes. Since I came to work for your father.' He took her hand and led her to a settee by the window. 'But you will call me Paul again, non?' he said as he sat down beside her. 'My home is in France where I have a château that I love very much, in Provence, and I very much wish to show it to you,' he added, his dark eyes looking deep into hers. He went on to talk easily of his home and Sam had time to take stock of him. His manner was charming and his French accent attractive, and these, coupled with his tall, lean good looks, made him a rather devastating person to be with. He paid her graceful and clever little compliments that brought a slight flush to her cheeks but didn't embarrass her and he seemed to take it for granted that they would be spending a lot of time together, saying that before she had shown him round Barbados, but now it would be his pleasure to show her.

Her father had been content to sit in the background while they talked, but during lunch he joined in the conversation more and Sam could see how much he enjoyed the company of the younger man, laughing and talking social chit-chat, but taking care to tell Sam who they were talking about.

'We must go to Sam Lord's Castle soon,' Paul was saying, and then, seeing Sam's puzzled frown, explained, 'That is a house that once belonged to a Regency buck called Sam Lord. It is said that he gained the fortune to build it by luring ships on to Cobblers Reef, but now it has been turned into a luxury hotel. You will come dancing there with me, will you not, *chérie*?'

Sam looked rather helplessly at her father and he smiled and nodded. 'Of course you must go. I want Samantha to go out a lot so that she forgets these last few weeks as soon as possible.'

Sam gripped her hands together under the table; did he really think that she would ever forget?

After lunch her father had to go back to his office, but Paul suggested a walk round the gardens and Sam joined him willingly enough. It was pleasant to have someone to talk to, someone who seemed to have time to spare for her and didn't have to rush away as her father did. Also Paul had travelled a lot and he talked so eloquently of the places he had visited that Sam's imagination was caught and she listened to him with interest. Also he sometimes made droll remarks that made her laugh and she found that the afternoon passed quickly and pleasantly, so that when he asked if he could call again tomorrow she readily agreed.

They turned to walk back to the house, passing between some bougainvillaea bushes near the surround-

ing wall that were a riot of mauve and purple flowers.
Suddenly a man whom Sam recognised as one of those
whom Mike had stunned stepped out in front of them
menacingly. He apologised at once as soon as he saw
who it was and moved back out of sight, but not before
Sam, with a sick feeling inside, had seen that he carried
a gun in a shoulder holster under his jacket.

Paul called to take her for a drive round the island
the next day but looked rather deprecatingly at the
American car he was driving. 'Shall we go in this or
would you prefer to take your own car?'

'My car?' Sam asked in surprise.

'Why, yes.' But then he raised his hands in a Gallic
gesture. '*Imbécile*! You must forgive me, *chérie*, I forgot that you might not have seen it yet. Come, I will
show you.'

He led the way round the side of the house to a court-
yard surrounded by garages that Sam hadn't seen before.
A black chauffeur who was washing down a limou-
sine turned to greet them and Paul said imperatively,
'Mademoiselle's car.'

The man jumped to push back the doors at one side
of the garages and Sam walked through, turning to
give the chauffeur a smile and a word of thanks. There
were four cars in the garage, but Paul led her to a low-
slung, Italian sports job that stood out like a jewel
among the more sedate sedans.

Sam gasped. 'You don't mean to tell me this is my
car?'

'But of course. It is beautiful, *n'est-ce pas*?' Paul said
enthusiastically. 'It is a De Tomaso Pantera. You can
get it up to a hundred and seventy-five miles an hour
on a straight run, but unfortunately there are few

roads on Barbados long enough for that,' he added regretfully.

He opened the driver's side door for her to get in, but Sam drew back. 'I can't sit there. I can't drive.'

'But of course you do, you are an excellent driver.'

'Oh, no, I—I just can't. Please, won't you drive?'

'Well, I will be pleased to, of course, but before——' he shrugged, 'well, you always hated anyone else to drive your car.'

'I did?' Sam's forehead creased into a frown. 'That— that must have been very selfish of me. But I certainly don't want to drive it now. Why, it looks more like a lethal weapon than a car.'

'Don't worry, *ma chère*, you will be quite safe with me.'

He helped her into the passenger seat and pushed back the sliding roof to let in some air. They drove sedately down the long drive flanked by lofty and graceful casuarina trees and through the iron gates. As they turned out into the road Sam saw another car coming out of the garage but took little notice of it. They turned north and headed up Highway One to the stretch that Paul told her was known as the Platinum Coast where the rich came only in the winter and which had now begun to be filled with large hotel complexes. Paul drove slowly through Speightstown where the streets still retained some of the atmosphere of earlier Barbados with their old colonial houses, the balconies overhanging the street and giving shade to hawkers who sold mangoes and limes from open trays while conversing animatedly with their neighbours.

As they drove further north the island became less

populated with correspondingly less traffic on the roads, and the countryside became a mass of fields of sugar cane with here and there a windmill turning busily in the trade winds, the 'winds of God' as the native Bajans called them. Paul pulled up at the extreme northern point of the island and for a while they stood and looked out at the miles and miles of open sea, but this reminded Sam too vividly of her time adrift in the dinghy with Mike and she turned hastily away.

'Come, you must see the Animal Flower Cave, it is one of the first places you took me to see,' Paul told her as he led the way towards a flight of stone steps.

The cave was really two caverns bored through the rock by centuries of pounding Atlantic waves at high tide. But now the tide was down and they could see the curious formations of stalactites and stalagmites and admire the reflection of the blue sky on the translucent pool in the far cavern. They sat on a rock and Paul told her the pools in the cave had once been an underwater garden of sea anemones, marine creatures that resembled flowers when their tiny tendrils were expanded so that the natives called them 'animal flowers'. And when anything came near them they withdrew their tendrils and became just an inconspicuous rubber-like tube, but generations of curious prodding fingers had discouraged them so that now they inhabited remote sea gardens in less accessible parts of the coast.

They were alone in the caverns and it was very quiet, the only sounds the gentle lapping of waves against stone. Paul put his arm across her shoulders, but Sam immediately drew away.

'No, please. Do not be afraid.' Paul's handsome face

looked at her intently. 'It is just that I must say something to you. But it is difficult for me to find the words.' He paused and then went on slowly, '*Chérie*, before —before you were taken away we had become very close, in fact we were on the point of announcing our engagement. No, do not say anything yet,' he added, lifting up a hand. 'I want you to know everything. It may be that you will meet others whom you used to know who will tell you that your father arranged the match. *Eh bien*, it is true that your father arranged that we should meet and would, I think, be very happy if we did marry, but, *chérie*, I want you to know that from the first moment we met we were attracted to one another.' He gave a half-rueful and very attractive smile. 'At first I was afraid to let you know how much I liked you, but when you let me see that you were not—how do you say it—indifferent to me, then I could contain myself no longer and told you how much I loved you.'

Sam flushed and sat up very straight, the memory of these same words said by another man searing into her brain. That man hadn't meant them, had used them as a weapon almost, but that didn't make Paul's avowal any more believable.

'I have told you this, *ma chère*, because it is a part of your past, I hope a very important part, and I think it is your right to know. But I also understand that now I am a stranger to you for whom you feel nothing. And I want you to know that I won't hold you to anything, that if in time you still feel nothing for me, that you have changed so much that even your old feelings are gone, then I will leave your father's employ and go away. I will not bother you again and even though I would be sad to leave you I would still be a very lucky man for I would have all the precious memories of our growing love and happiness, whereas you, *ma pauvre petite*, have had them taken from you.'

'Oh, Paul!' Sam looked at him, her eyes misty. 'Do you really mean it?'

'I give you my word,' he answered solemnly. 'And one thing more before we go. Your father is a very determined man, *chérie*; he loves you very much and it is his great ambition to see you married to someone deserving of your youth and beauty and, yes, position too, so it may be that he will try to coerce you into marrying either before you are ready to make a decision or even completely against your wishes. If he does then I want you to promise me that you will not try to face him alone, that you will tell me at once so that I can talk to him. And if he will not listen then I will leave so that he has no weapon with which to bully you.' He took her hands and held them. 'Will you promise me that, Samantha?'

Sam nodded gratefully. 'Oh, yes, Paul. And—and thank you.' She laughed a little. 'That's the first time you've called me by my name.'

He pulled a comically woeful face. 'It is very hard for a poor Frenchman to get his tongue round Samantha. So you will have to be content with *chérie*, I'm afraid.'

It was on the tip of her tongue to tell him to call her Sam, but something held her back. That was what Mike had called her; she could almost hear him now as he used to say her name on their island in a dozen different ways, sometimes exasperated, sometimes commanding, and sometimes—sometimes with his voice thick and breathless with desire. Damn it! Why did she always have to think of Mike? Abruptly she stood up and then shivered. Immediately Paul was contrite.

'But you are cold! I have kept you too long in these caverns. Come, let us go back into the sunlight at once.'

They emerged once more into the constant eighty degree heat and got into the car to continue their tour. As they pulled away another car fell in behind them and Sam recognised it as the one that had followed them from the house. She pointed it out to Paul.

He glanced in the driving mirror and shrugged. 'It is on your father's orders. They are to follow us to help protect you.'

Sam looked at him askance. 'You mean to say that I'm to be followed wherever I go?'

'You can hardly blame your father, *chérie*. It hit him very hard when you were kidnapped. He is terribly afraid that it might happen again, that it might give other people ideas. On the other hand he does not want to stop you having pleasure, to confine you to the house, so he does the best he can by providing you with as much protection as possible without restricting you in any way.' Paul's hand came out to cover hers. 'Believe me, *ma mie*, his only concern is for your happiness and safety.'

He squeezed her hand and held it until he had to put his own back on the wheel, and, almost to her own surprise, Sam didn't draw away. She felt overwhelmingly grateful to Paul; he was the only one who had shown any understanding of her feelings and difficulties. Both Mike and her father—Mike of course for his own reasons—had plunged her headlong into the relationships they had thrust upon her, explaining nothing, giving her no time to gradually build up the relationship again; even now her father had told her nothing of her mother, her grandparents or any other relatives, and he seemed to know next to nothing of any other of her friends except Paul, and spent little time at home. If he had wanted her back so badly why did he spend so little time with her? Sam thought resentfully, but then was immediately ashamed of herself; he had probably spent a great deal of time searching for her and now had to catch up with his work. And it must be a terrible responsibility running such a huge business empire.

So Sam was able to excuse him, and now that she had Paul to keep her company her father's absence wasn't so marked. Paul seemed to be able to devote as much time to her as he wanted, until Sam began to wonder just what his position was in her father's business, but these thoughts were pushed to the back of her mind because she was so glad to have his company. He was fun to be with, cheerful and always charming, and she was the recipient of several envious looks when he took her dancing at Sam Lord's turreted castle at Long Bay. Here they joined another couple whom she had known, and, although the conversation was necessarily stilted at times, she was pleased to think that she was picking up her old life again.

She met other friends when Paul took her racing in Bridgetown and to the Yacht Club, but he seemed to like to be alone with her and once or twice they spent the afternoon lying on the private beach a hundred yards or so from the house and screened from it by woodland. Here the white coral sand was soft as talcum powder underfoot and the water was warm and welcoming. Occasionally a fleet of bouffant clouds came cruising over the horizon, but somehow they never seemed to obscure the sun.

Sam liked the place so much that she began to go there every day alone, preferring it to the house where she somehow never seemed to be completely at ease; it was more of a showplace than a home. A raft had been anchored out in the sea and she often swam out to it to lie and sunbathe, but not in the nude; she was pretty sure that at least one of her father's guards was keeping an eye on her from the shade of the trees.

So one day she lay on her stomach on the raft while she flicked through the pages of a magazine, and contented herself by undoing the strap of the red bikini she was wearing so that her back would stay evenly brown. After a while a boat puttered slowly along quite a bit farther out to sea and anchored in the mouth of the bay. Sam glanced at it idly and saw a fishing line being cast from the stern, although the fisherman was hidden from her sight by the canopy. Uninterested, she returned to her magazine and presently dozed a little in the sun.

The raft rocked violently and Sam awoke with a start and then opened her mouth to scream at sight of the monster that was coming out of the sea towards her! But then a hand was clamped over her mouth and her heart gave a sickening jolt as she realised that it was a man in goggles and breathing apparatus, his oxygen tanks strapped on to his back. And even with all the scuba-diving paraphernalia obscuring his features she recognised him.

Mike said, 'Don't scream, Sam. Do you understand?'

She nodded and he removed his salty wet hand from her mouth. Holding on to the raft with one hand, he reached up to take off his goggles. His wet hair stuck damply to his forehead and drops of water clung to his eyelashes. He blinked them away and then his eyes, as blue as the sky, gazed intently at her face. 'Hi, sweetheart,' he said softly. 'You look better.' He lifted his right hand and gently stroked her cheek.

His touch brought Sam back to life. She trembled violently and drew away. 'Why did you have to come here? Don't you ever give up?' she asked bitterly.

His face hardened. 'Not where you're concerned. You happen to be all I have in the world that's worth fighting for.'

'Oh, Mike!' Sam shook her head in exasperated bewilderment. 'You're crazy. Don't you know that my father has men watching me all the time? There's one back on the beach now. If they catch you ...'

Mike gave a wry grin. 'Why do you think I chose this method? I've been sailing past here several times a day for the last week in the hope that I'd find you out here alone.'

'But why? What's the point?' She backed away from him. 'If you think you can carry me off again without me making a fuss, you're mistaken. The guard would inform the police and you'd be picked up within an hour. And don't think you can persuade me to go with you willingly, because I won't. I'm not going to let you dupe me again,' she added bitterly.

For a moment a bleak, fed-up look came into Mike's eyes, but then his jaw tightened and he said. 'That isn't why I'm here. I told you once before that I never forced myself on anyone; if you won't come with me of your own free will then I'm not going to make you. But I have to talk to you, tell you my side of what happened when we left Barbados. And that I think I have the right to demand of you.'

Sharply Sam retorted, 'You have no rights whatsoever where I'm concerned.'

Mike looked at her grimly. 'I seem to remember you saying that you owed your life to me. I don't like having to remind you of a debt, Sam, but in the circumstances I have no choice. You at least owe me the right to talk to you.'

Sam stared into his determined face unhappily, then shrugged. 'All right, go head. What do you want to say?'

'Not here,' Mike said rather wryly. 'It hardly makes a congenial venue for the things I have to tell you. You must meet me in Bridgetown tomorrow.'

'In Bridgetown? No, I won't! This is just another cheap trick to lure me away and ...'

Again his hand went over her mouth. 'Keep your voice down,' he warned. Their heads were very close and slowly he removed his hand and slipped it round the back of her neck. Deliberately he drew her head down to his and kissed her. For a moment she resisted, holding her head stiffly, but as she felt the warmth and sensuality of his mouth she slowly relaxed, her lips moving against his in a sudden, urgent need.

At last he let her go. 'You'll meet me tomorrow?'

Her eyes opened and she looked at him resentfully. 'Do you really think that using sex will make me do what you want?' she asked jeeringly.

'My poor Sam. Is that all you think it is?' His mouth suddenly broke into a broad grin. 'In that case I'd better

not tell you that your bikini top fell off five minutes
ago.'

'Oh!' Hastily Sam picked up the scrap of material
and put it back on. Then she sat up straight and looked
down at him with a frown on her face. 'Suppose I
do arrange to meet you—how do you know I won't
tell my father and let him have you arrested?'

'He can't, I haven't committed any crime—other
than marrying his daughter of course, which I must
admit is a crime in his eyes. He wanted to use you
in another way.'

'What do you mean—use me?'

'Well, I would call wanting to marry you off just to
further his business interests using you, wouldn't you?'
But he added quickly before she could speak, 'But
that's something we can talk about tomorrow. There
are a great many things about your old life that you
should know, things that I wanted to keep from you
if I could because we'd left them all behind us. But
your finding out who you were and going back to the
very place and people you were escaping from has
changed everything. Will you come?' he asked again.

'How can I be sure that you won't try to take me
away from my father again?'

Mike's eyes regarded her steadily. 'You'll just have
to trust me. Like I'll have to trust you not to bring
your father's henchmen to beat me up.'

Sam gazed into his face, remembering how she had
traced each feature with her fingers; the quizzical kink
in his eyebrows, the slight cleft in the firmness of his
chin, his lips. In little more than a murmur she said,
'What if I refuse to come?'

Mike's answer was said equally quietly but very

firmly. 'Then I shall have to find some other means of getting you alone.'

Her eyelids flew up at that and her eyes met his. 'How?'

'I shall come at night and climb into your room.'

Her voice sharp with alarm, she said at once, 'No! You mustn't. Mike, they have guns; promise me that you won't try it?'

'If you won't meet me any other way then I'll have to.'

She stared at him for a moment and then gave a tired sort of sigh. 'All right. Where do you want me to meet you?'

Matter-of-factly, and without any sign of triumph at her capitulation, he said, 'There's a wine bar in Swan Street called 'My Father's Moustache'. If you go into the big Da Costa's department store you'll find that there's a back entrance opening into Swan Street. The bar is a few yards down the road to the left. I'll be there at two in the afternoon.'

'What if I can't get rid of the guard?' Sam objected.

Mike grinned. 'You always managed to before.'

That shook her a little and she could only say uncertainly, 'But I might not be able to make it at two.'

'It doesn't matter, I'll wait all afternoon if I have to. And if you don't come tomorrow then I'll wait every day until you do,' he said forcefully.

Sam bit her lip and looked away, lost for words in the face of such strong resolution.

Mike glanced past her and then said warningly, 'Your watchdog has come on to the beach and is looking at my boat through his binoculars. I'll have to get back before he gets suspicious.'

'Can he see you?' Sam asked nervously, afraid to look round.

'No, you're hiding me from his view.'

He put on his goggles and was about to replace the mouthpiece of his air-tanks when Sam said urgently, 'Mike. Did—did my father hurt you when he threw you out of the house?'

Mike's mouth twisted wryly. 'I'm not a pretty sight where they kicked me in the ribs after they knocked me down the steps, but I managed to get away before they really started laying into me.' He saw the stricken look that came into her face and added reassuringly, 'Don't worry, sweetheart, I can take care of myself— and of you.'

And then he had slid silently back under the water and Sam had only a tell-tale trail of bubbles to watch until it was hidden by the waves. She lay down again and pretended to read and presently she saw the boat shake a little and then the fishing line reeled in, with, she saw with a touch of wry amusement, a biggish fish ostentatiously displayed at the end of the line. The boat's engine started up again and it moved slowly out of the bay back the way it had come, and when Sam glanced idly at the shore she saw the guard go back into the shade of the trees.

She lay there for an hour or so longer; there was no reason to hurry back to the house, Paul wouldn't be picking her up to take her out to dinner until seven, so there was plenty of time. Nervously she wondered how she was going to get away from her escort tomorrow afternoon. Mike had been so sure that she would manage it, and equally sure that she would keep her word and meet him. And rightly so, Sam reflected as she lay and gazed up at the deep blue of the sky, because, although she had raised a great many objections, she had known right from the moment he had kissed her that she would do as he asked.

CHAPTER SEVEN

THE sun was high in the sky overhead when Sam had herself driven into the capital the next day. The chauffeur pulled up in a car park near the bus park and she told him to come back and collect her at five. Another car had drawn up nearby and two men got out of it, looking out of place in jackets that concealed their shoulder holsters when everyone else was in casual, short-sleeved shirts. But even the men and nerves about what she was about to do were forgotten for a while as Sam looked about her in fascinated curiosity. This part of the town was busy with people who arrived from the north of the island on buses which were open at both sides and painted bright red or yellow. The buses came and went at intervals, manoeuvring their way carefully between groups of women carrying loaded trays balanced by cloth pads on their heads. Other women squatted on small portable wooden benches and tried to tempt passers-by to buy popcorn, coconut cakes, peanuts or fruit. And further along the car park an open-air barber was shearing the heads of grinning customers right down to the scalp, and under the spreading evergreen trees other men played dominoes while they waited their turn.

Taking her time, Sam walked slowly along, stopping to look in shop windows and to make one or two small purchases, the men always just a few paces behind her, their eyes alert, their hands free to grab at their guns if necessary. Sam began to tremble a little and her hands felt clammy so that she had to take out her handkerchief and wipe them, but she walked resolutely on, drawing nearer to the centre of the town. As she neared the entrance to Da Costa's, the Selfridges of Bridgetown, she glanced back and saw that the men were still close behind but looking bored and somewhat fagged now from the heat.

The interior of the store, however, was air-conditioned and she was able to look round the counters in comfort. Her guards, too, must have appreciated the cooler atmosphere, but it was obvious from the wistful glances they cast in the direction of a cafeteria that they were dying for a drink to quench their thirst. And this gave Sam an idea when she went to the dress department and saw that there was a bar on the same floor. She took a long time pretending to examine the rows of dresses while keeping an eye as unobtrusively as possible on the two men. At last they succumbed to temptation and one went off to get a drink. When they changed over Sam was ready. As soon as they turned to speak to each other she ducked down below the level of the clothes racks and ran through an archway into another department where she pushed open the door to the service stairs, leaving it swinging. Then she dodged out of sight as the men came running in to look for her and naturally assumed that she'd gone through the door. They dashed down the stairway and Sam calmly walked back through the store, took a lift down to ground level, and turned out into Swan Street. The wine bar was just a short way along and she found Mike waiting for her in a booth near the doorway.

He stood up as she came in and a light came into his eyes that made her heart give a crazy kind of jolt. He didn't speak but took her hand and led her through the bar and out into a sort of service road where a car was waiting. He opened the door for her, but Sam held back, her face suddenly tense.

Mike said reassuringly, 'It's all right, I'm not trying to pull anything. There was always the chance that those men might have found us if we'd stayed in the bar, and I don't want there to be any interruptions when we talk. This is too important. Here,' he held out a bunch of keys. 'If it makes you feel any better you can drive.'

Slowly Sam shook her head. 'No, you drive.' She got into the car and Mike folded himself in beside her. He made the car look very small.

He grinned. 'That's the first time I've ever heard you offer to let anyone else drive. It was the only thing you used to get mad with me about—the fact that I insisted on doing the driving.'

'Even in my car?'

'Your Italian sports job? Yes, even in that. It's just one of those things a man does better than a woman.'

A shade defiantly, Sam said, 'Someone told me I was a very good driver.'

Mike glanced sideways at her as he drove out of town. 'Was?'

'Yes. I—I've forgotten how,' she confessed. 'Like swimming, I suppose.'

'But you picked that up again quickly enough.'

'Only because you made me go in the water and gave me my confidence back.'

Mike's voice hardened. 'And hasn't Paul de Lacey restored your confidence to drive? Even though he's obviously been paying you fulsome compliments?'

'They weren't *fulsome* compliments,' Sam began angrily, and then stopped, realising she'd walked neatly into his trap. She flushed, and said, 'So you know about him?'

'Of course. Your father imported him into the island as the latest suitor for your fortune about three months before I met you.'

Tartly Sam said, 'It isn't my fortune that he's interested in.'

He was about to make a somewhat scathing retort, but when he saw her flushed face, Mike said merely, 'We'll talk about it later,' and drove on in silence.

At length they came in sight of the sea again and Mike pulled off the road down a track that led to a clearing fringed by a riot of flowering trees: jacarandas, frangipani, and, most brilliant of all, the flame red flamboyants.

'Let's take a walk, shall we?' He got out of the car and waited for her.

Slowly Sam joined him. He was wearing a casual blue linen shirt with the cuffs turned back and slacks of a darker shade. A yearning that was like a physical pain suddenly filled her and she had to turn hastily away and walk ahead of him along a path that led them to the edge of the cliffs overlooking the sea. They found a fallen tree trunk to sit on and for a while they sat in silence. But it wasn't a pleasant silence; because

of that sudden wave of sexuality Sam now felt tense
and ill at ease, sitting so that there was a definite
gap between them. Above their heads great casuarinas
swayed and sighed in the trade winds and flurries of
leaves drifted over them in lemon-drop showers, but
for once the beauty of the scene was lost on Sam, she
could think of nothing but the man who sat so silently
beside her.

When she could stand it no longer she said sharply,
'I thought you wanted to talk to me?'

Mike turned to her and she was surprised to see a
somewhat sad look in his eyes, but then he said, 'All
right, I'll give it to you from the beginning. But you'll
have to be tough, Sam, because what I have to say is
going to hurt.' He paused a moment, but when she
didn't speak went on, 'I first met you about ten weeks
before we got married. You'd spent the evening with a
crowd of people at the Pepper Pot, that's a swank night-
club in Bridgetown. When I found you, you were alone
on the beach in the early hours of the morning, you'd
had far too much to drink and you were about to walk
out into the sea.'

Sam looked at him frowningly. 'Go for a swim, you
mean?'

'No, I don't,' he answered bluntly. ' I meant that you
were going to try to drown yourself. Just swim out so
far that you wouldn't have enough strength to get
back even if you changed your mind.'

Appalled, Sam said immediately, 'That isn't true,
I wouldn't do such a thing. You're lying again!'

She went to get up, but Mike pulled her down again.
'Hear me out, Sam. I told you this was going to be
tough.' Keeping a hold of her arm, he continued, 'I

saw you from my boat and went in the water after you. You fought like a wildcat and I had to hit you before I could get you out. I took you to the boat and just dumped you on a bunk to recover while I changed into dry clothes and patched up the scratches you'd torn in my face.' He shook his head in remembered anger. 'God, I was mad at you. I thought you were some dumb, drunken, kid who'd had a row with her boy-friend and wanted to draw attention to herself.' His voice softened. 'But then you came round and I saw the hurt and misery in your eyes and realised that the drink was just to give you the courage to commit suicide.'

'No!' Actually hearing him say the word made it all seem more terrible.

His eyes flickered over her. 'It's true, Sam. You were in a hell of a state and you desperately needed a shoulder to cry on. Well, mine are pretty broad and, after I'd made you get out of your wet clothes, you just sat there wrapped in my beach robe and drinking coffee and told me everything.'

'What? What did I tell you?'

Mike didn't spare her any. 'How your father's over-powering ambition was ruining your life. How when you were only eighteen he forced you to become en-gaged to the son of a wealthy American businessman, except the son turned out to be a drug addict who tried to get you hooked on to the stuff, only he took a walk out of a twenty-second-floor window. Then your father tried to fix you up with some Arabian oil magnate and when you rebelled at that tried instead to make you accept a man nearly old enough to be your grandfather who was one of his biggest rivals.

So to foil him you got engaged to a boy-friend instead, then broke it off when the boy started pressing you to set a date. And so it went on, until Paul de Lacey came to work for your father and you thought you'd found someone who wanted you only for yourself at last.'

Sam gazed at him, her eyes wide and dark in her set face. In little more than a whisper she said, 'Go on.'

Mike looked at her, hating to see the hurt in her eyes, but knowing that he had to do it for her own sake. 'You were happy, very happy, for a few months, but then, the night I found you, you overheard something you weren't meant to hear and you found out that your father was paying de Lacey to marry you.'

'Oh, no! Mike, he isn't like that.'

His voice harsh, Mike said, 'You overheard him discussing a marriage contract with your father. He was to be paid a lump sum as soon as the ceremony took place. And Paul de Lacey was trying to push the price up because he'd found out your mother committed suicide. They tried to hush it up and gave out that she'd got cramp while swimming, but de Lacey had found out the truth.'

'She—she drowned herself?' The sky and the sea suddenly seemed to merge and Sam had to grip hard on the log to stop herself from fainting.

'Yes. I'm sorry, sweetheart.' He tried to take her hand, but Sam snatched it away. He said heavily, 'I knew that you wouldn't take my word for it, so I got you these.' He went to the car and brought back a bulky envelope which he gave to her.

Slowly Sam opened it and found inside a sheaf of photostats, all of newspaper items. There were photographs with the announcement of her first engagement and, dated a few months later, a story on her fiancé's death, then other items, mostly sensationalist, about other on-off romances, including a picture of her with Paul headlined, 'ASHBY HEIRESS AND FRENCH PLAYBOY'. And lastly there was an extract from an English newspaper dated over ten years ago giving a brief account of her mother's death by drowning, with the cryptic footnote, 'the coroner brought in an open verdict as Mrs Ashby was partially clothed at the time'.

Sam dropped the photostats as if they were scalding her and stood up abruptly. She turned and walked a few yards away from him to lean her head against a tamarind tree. The scent of bougainvillaea filled her nostrils and humming birds darted among the trees like metallic bees. Mike's hands came on her shoulders, but she didn't turn to him.

'Is that all you have to tell me?'

'No, I wanted to tell you about us.' He hesitated. 'But if you don't feel that you can take any more today ...'

Sam's voice was suddenly harsh. 'For God's sake say what you have to say!'

'All right.' He turned her round to face him. 'After I fished you out of the sea you used to come and visit me on the boat. At first I thought it was just because it was something different for you, a diversion for the poor little rich girl, and I tried to get rid of you. You represented the kind of complication I didn't want in my life. But you seemed to enjoy messing about on the boat and trying your hand at cooking in the galley. You were forever giving your father's men the slip and coming on board when my back was turned. You were a very stubborn young woman.'

His face changed then and when he raised his eyes
to look at her his gaze was physical. He reached and
took her hands, turning them over in his big palms,
studying them reflectively. His thumb caressed her bare
ring finger gently. 'And then I had to admit that I
liked having you around. So I went to your father and
told him I wanted to marry you.' His lips thinned. 'He
asked me how much money I wanted to clear out and
leave you alone. So it was then you decided that you
just couldn't take any more and that we'd just get
married and go. We were sitting here, right on that log,
when you said it. I was hoping that coming here would
bring it back so I wouldn't have to put you through
all this.'

Sam looked at the flower-strewn clearing and said
huskily, 'Can you prove that we were married, Mike?'
And her hands trembled in his.

He answered forcefully, 'The church where we were
married is only half an hour's drive from here. You can
look in the register we signed and talk to the priest.
He may even know the people we brought in as witnesses, although they were strangers to us, just two
native Bajans who happened to be passing.' His grip
tightened. 'Will you come, Sam?'

Slowly she straightened up and squared her shoulders. 'Yes, all right, I'll come with you.'

They drove on further north through the endless
acres of sugar cane and presently Mike pulled up beside a small house set among trees at the foot of a hill,
and at the top of the hill there was a small stone church
that looked out across the ocean towards the beloved
homeland of the Scottish exiles who had built it.

'Why don't you go on up?' Mike suggested. 'I'll find the priest and follow you.'

Sam nodded and began to climb the steep track, the breeze catching at her skirt. At the door of the church she paused and looked at the waves pounding against the cliffs, the noise loud in her ears. And even when she pushed open the heavy wooden doors and went inside she could still hear it, but now it was no longer a pounding roar, only a muted sigh that emphasised the stillness and quiet of the little church.

It was just as Mike had described it, with the sun shining through the stained glass windows, but even his vivid description hadn't prepared her for the sense of peace and tranquillity that stole over her as she walked slowly up the aisle and gazed at the simple altar with the plain wooden cross above it. A feeling of familiarity came to her for the first time since she had lost her memory and she seized on it eagerly, trying to force memory back, but the more she tried the more elusive it became. Desperately she looked around the church, almost convincing herself that she could remember it full of flowers and with two native workers as their witnesses, but then she gave an angry sigh and sat down in one of the front pews; she was getting so confused that she was mistaking imagination for truth.

When Mike came in five minutes later she was still sitting there and looked up quickly, but he shook his head.

'The priest is out at the moment, but they're sending a boy to fetch him. It shouldn't take long.'

'Can we look at the register while we're waiting?'

'I'm afraid not, he keeps it locked up.' He came to

sit beside her and put his arm along the back of the pew. 'Does being here bring anything back to you?'

'No.' Sam shook her head. 'For a moment I—I felt that there *was* something, but I think it was more the atmosphere of the church that was familiar rather than the place itself or anything that happened here.' She looked down at her hands. 'I'm sorry, I know it sounds ridiculous.'

His hand dropped on to her shoulder, warm and strong. 'It's a start, Sam. You're doing fine. Maybe more will come with time.'

Terribly aware of him so close to her, Sam said rather unsteadily, 'Are you—are you living on the boat you bought in St Vincent?'

'No, I let the deal fall through when you—when you left. I needed to get back to Barbados quicker than a boat could take me. I have a room at the Miramar Hotel further up the Platinum Coast from your father's place.'

'Oh, I see.'

It seemed an incongruous kind of conversation to have in such a place and Mike must have felt it too, because he turned to her, his face serious, and began, 'Sam, there's something I have to know,' but was interrupted when the church door opened and the priest, a European, came in.

Mike looked at him in some surprise. 'I'm sorry, they must have sent the boy for the wrong person. It was the Reverend Mr Maddox we wanted to see.'

'You're just too late for him, I'm afraid,' the priest said as he came forward to shake hands with Mike. 'He left a few days ago to go back to England. I'm taking over the parish until a new priest can be appointed.'

'Went back to England?' Mike said sharply. 'But why? Why did he go back?'

The priest looked at him, surprised at his urgency, but said goodnaturedly, 'Something to do with a family matter, I believe. It was all a bit sudden, you know. But I think you said you wanted to look in the register. I can at least help you there.' He took a key from his pocket and led them towards the tiny vestry.

Slowly Sam followed, with Mike, his face gone suddenly tense, close behind her. The priest found the book for them and Mike told him the date they wanted. He opened it and put on a pair of glasses to find the place, his fingers fumbling and slow. At last he straightened up.

'Doesn't seem to be anything here for that date, I'm afraid. Nothing in that month except a baptism on the nineteenth.'

'There must be. Here, let me look.' Impatiently Mike took the book from him and examined it, turning several of the pages. Then he looked at it more closely and his face grew grim. 'A page has been cut out of here with a razor blade,' he said harshly.

'What? But that's most irregular.' The priest looked and had to agree with him. 'I must report this to the bishop at once,' he muttered, and locked the book up again before hurrying away and leaving them alone.

Sam had been standing silently by while they had been talking, but now she turned on her heel and started to walk out of the church.

Mike caught her arm and spun her round. 'Sam, wait.'

She stared at him, her face white and tense. 'Why, so that you can think up another load of lies to tell me? Did you really think I would fall for all this, Mike? A priest suddenly called away, a page cut out of a book? I may have lost my memory, but that doesn't make me an idiot!'

She went to pull away from him, but his grip tightened. 'Think about it, Sam. Who would want to hide all traces of our marriage?'

'You're not trying to say it was my father? He wouldn't go to those lengths to ...'

'Oh, yes, he would, Sam. Your father is the kind of man who's ruthless enough to go to any lengths to get what he wants.'

'You're crazy! How could he have a clergyman recalled to England?'

'It's simple enough if you have sufficient money to hire a detective agency to find out about his relations and then send a telegram saying that one of them is ill and needs him.'

Sam gazed at him in disbelief. 'You know something, Mike, you have a warped mind. My father didn't even know where we were supposed to have got married. And I couldn't have told him, because I didn't know exactly where myself.'

At that Mike's voice began to grow angry. 'There's no supposed about it. You told him we got married before we left Barbados, didn't you? All he had to do was to have enquiries made at all the likely churches until he found the right one, then cut out the page in the register and get rid of the priest. Easy enough when you have absolutely no scruples.'

Sam's eyes glittered angrily in her pale face. 'And just as easy for *you* to find a church where the priest was recently called away and for you to cut a page out of the book and pretend it was the one with our names on! You're the one without any scruples, Mike Scott!'

She tried to break free of his grip, but he pulled her roughly against him and held her by both wrists.

'What about the newspaper clippings I showed you, doesn't that prove I'm telling you the truth?'

'About my past, yes, but not about the interpretation you put on it. It doesn't have to have been my father's fault that I got engaged to the wrong man or—or had my name linked with others. I might have been that type of person, someone who couldn't settle down until the right man came along. And that man could have been Paul. There was nothing to prove that my father put him up to it. I have only your word for that—and just what is that worth?' she added nastily. 'The word of a kidnapper and a rapist!'

Mike's face had grown suddenly pale under his tan. 'I ought to knock your head off for saying that,' he said fiercely.

But Sam hardly heard him as she swept on, 'And if my life with my father was so terrible why did I stay with him, live in the same house—answer me that?'

He glared down at her. 'Because you loved him, of course. Because he kept telling you he only wanted the best for you, that you were all he had. And you kept making excuses for him and hoping he'd eventually give up on you and let you lead your own life. And it wasn't until you found out that his jealousy and ruthlessness had driven your mother to her death that you finally realised he'd never change. And that near enough broke you up.'

His voice softened, but Sam refused to listen. 'You

have no proof of that, just as you have no proof that
I even knew you before you took me away from my
father. You've bent all the facts to suit your own story.
You're trying to make me so confused and mixed up
that I won't know who to believe. But all your lies
have had the opposite effect to what you wanted, because I like Paul and if he asks me to marry him again
I shall!'

A look of absolute fury came into Mike's eyes and he
gripped her wrists painfully hard as she struggled to
get free. 'And our baby?' he said savagely. 'Are you
going to let him believe it's his?'

Sam suddenly became very still. All the angry colour
drained from her cheeks leaving her ashen-faced. 'You
—you knew about that?' she whispered.

'Of course I knew. I can count as well as you can.'
He waited for her to speak, but when she didn't he said
more gently, 'I've been waiting for an opportunity to
talk to you about it, make plans. We'll have to decide
on somewhere to live and ...'

'No!' She looked away, unable to meet his eyes.

'All right, if you don't want to discuss it here, but ...'

'I won't want to talk about it at all. There's nothing to discuss,' she said abruptly.

'What do you mean?' A sudden flame of savage anger
came into his eyes and he yanked her round to face him,
his fingers biting cruelly into her flesh. 'Are you trying
to tell me that you killed it? That you destroyed our
baby?' He began to shake her violently. 'Answer me,
Sam. Answer me!' he yelled at her.

'Yes, they gave me some pills to take, but I ...' But
he was shaking her so hard that her teeth rattled.

'You let them do a thing like that to you? You let them kill it?'

'I didn't know. I didn't realise!' She had to shout to make herself heard above his fury and suddenly she found that she was crying, great racking sobs as tears poured down her cheeks.

And then she was in Mike's arms and he was holding her very tight. 'It's all right, Sam. It's all right. I'm sorry. I know you wouldn't deliberately do a thing like that. Oh, God, what a hell of a mess!'

He buried his face in her hair and held her close against him. Sam closed her eyes tightly and just let herself take in the wonderful feeling of being back in his arms. Here for a moment she found the security and comfort she so desperately needed. His strength and warmth were like a shield that could guard her from all the doubts and fears that beset her. If only she could believe in him, know for sure that he was telling the truth. She looked up and saw the tender light in his eyes, but then her own eyes dilated as she saw a hand bring a gun butt savagely down on Mike's head. He gave a spasmodic jerk and then fell unconscious at her feet.

Sam stared in stunned horror as the bodyguard she thought she'd lost in Bridgetown again brought his gun down on Mike's head and a bright trickle of blood began to spread over the stone floor.

'No! Leave him alone!' She threw herself forward as he pushed Mike over with his foot and went to bring the weapon down to smash his face. The gun landed on her arm and she gave a cry of pain, but the next minute she was pulled off Mike by the other bodyguard who began to drag her outside. Immediately Sam

started to struggle and scream at the top of her voice
and the man with the gun gave a curse and came to
help quieten her. They half carried her down the slope
to their car and thrust her inside just as the priest came
running out of his house. She tried to call to him, to
tell him to go to Mike, but one of the men put his
hand over her mouth and pushed her down into the
seat while the other started the car and they drove
away.

They had gone some distance before the man let her
go and then she sat up and glared at him furiously.
'How *dare* you manhandle me? I'm going to tell my
father about you and get you thrown out!'

He looked at her jeeringly. 'It wasn't our fault if you
got knocked about a bit when we were trying to save
you from being kidnapped again.'

'He wasn't trying to kidnap me,' she retorted indig-
nantly.

'No? Then perhaps your father would be interested
to know that you deliberately gave us the slip again
so that you could go and meet him,' the man said
leeringly.

Sam gazed at him in consternation, then bit her lip
and looked away as he laughed scornfully. But after
a while she said, 'How did you know where to look for
me?'

He shrugged. 'We thought he might try to take you
back there.'

'Oh, why should he do that?' Sam tried to keep her
voice indifferent, but he must have realised where her
questions were heading and rudely told her to mind
her own business.

Sam sat back against the cushioned seat, trying to

work out if they'd gone to the church because they
knew that Mike might take her there to try to bring
back her memory—if they had really been married
there—in which case the men themselves might have
been there before to cut out the page from the register.
Her head began to pound as she tried to sort out fact
from fiction, but it was all too much of a muddle and
she eventually gave up, leaning against the seat ex-
haustedly. Worriedly she wondered if Mike had been
badly hurt; the man had hit him so hard. She remembered his white face and the blood staining the stones
and a cold feeling of fear and helplessness swamped
her. She had to know how he was, but how to find out
when she was watched the whole time? But then she
realised that the clergyman would know, she had only
to telephone him when she got back to the house
and he would be able to tell her how Mike was.

That thought gave her some comfort and she sat
quietly until they drew up outside the house, then she
ran in without a backward glance and hurried up to
her room. There was an extension telephone there,
but even as she went to pick it up she realised that
she didn't know what number to ring or how to get
hold of the operator to find the number for her. She
had a quick search round the desk in her sitting room
but couldn't find any directories. Darn! Sam bit her
fingertip in perplexity and then thought that she would
probably find what she wanted in her father's study,
so she hurried downstairs again.

The directory was in the drawer of his desk and Sam
sat down to search for the number. She supposed it
would be under the name of the Reverend Mr Maddox. But as she searched she was surprised to hear

her father's voice as he came into the adjoining drawing-room, the connecting door to which was standing open. He was speaking to Mrs Gregory, the housekeeper, and Sam expected them to be discussing some domestic matter and so she was amazed to hear the woman say, pleadingly, 'James darling, you haven't come to me for three nights now. Promise me you'll come tonight. You know how much I need you.'

Her father laughed. 'You can never get enough, can you? But you knew from the start that you wouldn't be the only woman in my life. If I choose to go elsewhere for my entertainment, that's my business.'

'Oh, James, you're so cruel to me. You know I love you. When will you let me get a divorce so that we can be married?'

'I thought your husband refused to give you a divorce?'

The housekeeper's voice was eager now. 'He would if you paid him enough, I know he would. He only wants more money.'

'Oh, sure. There isn't anyone who won't do what you want if you pay them enough—except one,' he added, his voice thoughtful.

'Then you'll do it?'

'No.' His tone was decisive. 'I've already told you that I won't contemplate marriage or even acknowledge you as my mistress until Samantha is safely married. I don't want even the breath of any more scandal to mar her chances with the Comte de Lacey. He's already ...'

But what he was about to say was cut off as Mrs Gregory said petulantly, 'Oh, Samantha! It's always Samantha. She always comes first. Nothing's ever allowed to harm her even though she threw everything you've done for her back in your face by run ... Oh!' Sam heard her give a sudden exclamation of pain. 'James, don't, you're hurting me!'

'Then leave my daughter out of it. You're not fit to even clean her shoes. I don't know why the hell I keep you around.'

'Yes, you do.' Her tone was soft and honeyed now. 'You keep me here because there's no one else who can give you what you want as well as I do. Come to me tonight and I'll prove it to you. Like this ...'

Her voice trailed off and Sam quietly slipped the directory back into the drawer, then went to the door and opened it and then closed it again, making as much noise about it as she could, and at the same time calling out, 'Daddy? Are you there?'

Immediately her father replied from the drawing-room. 'I'm in here, Samantha. Be with you in just a minute.'

Sam turned to look out of the window and heard the door of the drawing-room softly close and then her father came into the study, smoothing back his hair.

He smiled. 'Hello, my dear, what can I do for you?'

Sam looked at him steadily. 'You can talk to me, please. You can tell me all the things I've wanted to know about myself ever since you brought me back here.'

'Oh?' He eyed her warily. 'What did you want to know?'

He sat down at his desk and Sam came to stand in front of it, her hands gripping the edge. Tersely she said, 'I want to know how my mother died. And I want to know how you allowed me to be engaged to a drug addict and when he died tried to marry me off to further your business interests. And I want to know whether you're paying Paul de Lacey to—to court me now. But most of all,' she leaned forward to emphasise her words, 'most of all,' she repeated, 'I want to know the truth about Mike Scott.'

Her father stared at her. 'Who's been talking to you?'

'That doesn't matter. Now it's *you* who's going to do the talking—and I want the truth, the whole truth.'

For a moment longer he gazed at her, then he sat back, apparently at ease. He gave a rather tired sigh. 'All right, Samantha, if that's the way you want it, although I must confess that I'd hoped to keep all this from you.' He steepled his fingers together and began slowly, 'Your mother died from drowning; it was purely accidental, but there was some nasty, malicious gossip at the time because, I'm grieved to have to admit, we had been going through a bad patch in our marriage. But we'd got over that and everything was fine again. Her death was a terrible shock, to both of us, and that's why I moved out here, to get away from unhappy memories—and from the gossip,' he added bitterly.

'As for your first boy-friend, you met him when you were at college in America and you refused to listen to all reason and went ahead and got engaged against my wishes. You are—or rather you were—an extremely headstrong person, young lady. You seem to have changed quite a bit, and for the better, I might add. And as for trying to marry you off——!' He laughed. 'Trying to make you do anything against your will was worse than bashing my head against a brick wall. No, you naturally met many of my business associates at parties and other gatherings and the gossip columnists seized on even the most unlikely people as the next candidate for your hand. Admittedly you made mistakes, you got engaged a couple of times more, but they didn't last long, as soon as you realised that half the attraction was my money you dropped them out of your life. It was only natural, Samantha, and I was partly to blame, I was so wrapped up in my work that I didn't give you enough of myself, and without a mother to guide you ...' He shrugged expressively.

'And Paul, you haven't told me about him? Is he a fortune-hunter?'

Her father laughed. 'Hardly. He's got a pedigree that goes back into the beginnings of history and he owns a large estate in France with a huge and ancient château. And he's connected to half the wealthy and noble families in France either by blood or marriage. No, Samantha, it's the opposite way round. He came over to learn a bit more about big business politics from me and only intended to stop a couple of months before going back to Paris, but then he met you and stayed on. He doesn't need money, and he's one of the most eligible bachelors in Europe.' He looked at her quizzically. 'Have I answered all your questions now?'

'All—all except one.' Sam looked at him searchingly. 'You haven't told me about Mike.'

'Mike Scott.' Her father's lips set into a grim sneer. 'He's nothing but an opportunist. I suppose he must have read about you in the papers or had you pointed out to him somewhere and worked out a plan to kidnap you, trying to make it look as if you'd gone with him willingly. The police found out that you received a telephone call just before you left the house and they think you were lured out on some pretext; as you've lost your memory we shall never know. But because of the kind of man he is he was suspected from the start.'

'What do you mean, the kind of man he is?'

Her father looked at her steadily. 'He's a drop-out,' he said bluntly. 'He had a thriving business going in England, was on the point of becoming a millionaire, but he suddenly gave it all up and came out to the West Indies to become a beachcomber. Just bought himself a boat to live on and went native. The only work he ever does is occasionally to hire himself and the boat out to deep-sea fishermen. He's a failure, Samantha, no good to you or any woman.'

'But if he sold his business why should he need money?' Sam protested.

'He didn't sell it. He just left it in the hands of the directors.' James Ashby shook his head. 'The man must be crazy. He could have been something really big by now. Unless it was found out that he'd done some shady deals or been milking the company and got kicked out,' he added derisively. 'It wouldn't surprise me at all. He's just a parasite, Samantha, one of the thousands who cling on to the wealthy for what they can get out of them, fawning sycophants who spit at you behind your back and tell you they're your best friend to your face. I know, I've seen enough of them—and Mike Scott is one of the worst kind. If you hadn't made me promise to leave him alone, he'd be serving a twenty-year sentence by now.'

'And you're sure that I didn't know him before he kidnapped me?'

'Quite certain, if you had I would have known about it.'

'I see.' Sam stood up and said formally, 'Thank you

for telling me. I hope I haven't kept you from anything important.'

Her father looked at her then stood up and came to place his hands on her shoulders. Earnestly he said, 'Nothing is more important than you, Samantha. All I have, everything I do, it's all for you, you know. And I want you to feel that you can come to me at any time and with any problem.' He kissed her on the forehead. 'All right?'

'Yes, of course,' Sam answered rather woodenly. 'If you'll excuse me I'd better go and change.'

'A date with Paul?'

'Yes, he's taking me out to dinner at La Bonne Auberge in St Philip.'

'Sounds great, have a good time.'

Sam nodded and then went quickly upstairs again. A worried glance at her watch told her that it was now over two hours since the attack on Mike and she still hadn't got the priest's number. Perhaps it might be better if she phoned his hotel direct, he might be back there by now. Or in a hospital, she thought with rising anxiety. She got her maid to tell her how to get the operator and then asked for the Miramar Hotel. Impatiently she waited while the operator looked up the number and put her through. The phone seemed to ring for a long time in Mike's room and she was almost on the point of putting it down so that she could try and contact the priest when to her vast relief she heard his voice.

'Mike! Mike, are you all right?'

'Sam? Yes, I'm okay. Where are you?'

'At the house. When you didn't answer I thought— I thought you must be in hospital.'

'No, I was bathing the cut when you rang.'

'That's all it was? It looked so terrible.'

'Forget about it. I'm all right. I take it it was your father's thugs?'

'Yes. One of them hit you with his gun butt.'

'You must point him out to me,' Mike said grimly. 'I'd like a word or two with him.' But then he added more gently, 'Sam, about this afternoon . . .'

But she broke in quickly, 'I've talked to my father, asked him about the things you told me.'

'And?'

'And he's taken every fact and shown it to me in a different light, in a way that completely exonerates him of blame.'

She heard him swear under his breath. Then, 'Sam, you've got to believe me, if you . . .'

'Why? Why should I believe you rather than him?' Her voice rose angrily. 'And quite frankly, as of right now I don't really care which of you is telling the truth!' And she slammed down the receiver.

CHAPTER EIGHT

WHEN Paul came to meet her that night, looking extremely handsome in a well-cut tuxedo, he drew her into the library before they left the house and firmly closed the door.

'Before we go out I have something for you,' he said with his charming smile. 'Now you must close your eyes and you must promise me not to open them until I say, *tu comprends?*'

He looked so mysterious that Sam laughingly obeyed him. She felt him come up behind her and then place something cold and rather heavy about her neck. She reached up to touch it, but he stopped her. 'Mais non, you must wait until I give you permission.' He took hold of her arm and led her forward, positioning her so that when he said, 'Now, you may open your eyes,' she was facing directly into a mirror.

The necklace was brilliant and scintillating, it hung round her neck like a thing alive, a sparkling river of diamonds and emeralds that outshone even the green in her eyes. Slowly Sam lifted her hand to touch it.

'It—it can't be real!' she breathed.

Paul looked pained. 'But of course it is real. Do you think that I would insult beauty such as yours by giving you imitation jewellery?'

Immediately Sam was contrite. 'I'm sorry, I didn't mean to offend you. I just can't believe—it's so beautiful, so—so overwhelming!'

He smiled. 'I am glad you like it.' He came to stand behind her and put his hands lightly on her shoulders. 'It belonged to an ancestress of mine who was one of Marie Antoinette's ladies in waiting. Her portrait hangs in my home in France. She too was very lovely, and I think she would approve of your having her necklace.'

For a while the sheer magnificence of the jewels had driven all other thoughts out of her head, but now she looked at him with a slight frown. 'But I don't understand? You surely don't mean—you did only bring it to show me, didn't you?'

His hands began to caress her bare shoulders. 'But no, ma mie, it is for you, a gift. A small token which can only indicate a fraction of what I feel for you.

Oh, *chérie*!' He went to turn her into his arms, but Sam stepped quickly away, putting up her hands to try and undo the clasp of the necklace.

Agitatedly she said, 'But I can't take it, you know I can't. You had no right to give it to me after you said you wouldn't push yourself on me.' Her fingers fumbled at the unfamiliar catch. 'Oh, darn, I can't get it undone.'

Paul chuckled softly and came to pull her hands down. 'Then you will just have to wear it, won't you? And perhaps by the time this evening is over I will have persuaded you to give me the right to smother you in jewels.'

Sam tried to protest further, but he wouldn't listen, taking her hand and leading her out to the car. And all that evening he put himself out to be even more charming to her if that were possible, and the result was devastating; he seemed to have eyes for no one else but her, behaved towards her as if she was the only woman in the whole crowded room, and overwhelmed her by his sheer self-confidence and attentiveness. When they danced he held her close, moulding her against him, and when they drank the champagne he ordered, he lifted his glass to her in a silent but eloquent toast.

After their meal Paul took her on to a night club and they stayed there very late, dancing to a slow, smoochy group on a pocket-sized dance floor, until they were almost the last couple in the place. Only then did Paul put her stole round her shoulders and lead her out to the car. He drove along beside the coast for a few miles and then down a narrow track that took them to a deserted cove, the sand glistening like silver in the moonlight. He helped Sam out and they walked along beside the water's edge, the sound of the waves lapping gently against the shore, their tips a phosphorescent glow beneath the breathtaking radiance of the moon. Behind them, in the stretch of woodland leading to the beach, tree frogs made a clinking sound and other frogs took up the cry until their collected voices sounded like glass chandeliers jangling gently in the breeze.

The night had an almost soporific effect on Sam, she felt emotionally drained by the events of the day, but she'd drunk enough champagne to blunt the rawness of her nerves and now she felt only tired and unwilling to face tomorrow. She'd had enough conflict and was grateful to Paul for giving her the chance to forget her problems, even for a few hours.

He was walking along beside her, his arm casually round her waist, but presently he stopped and turned her round to face him.

'Ah, *chérie*, how lovely you look in the moonlight,' he said softly. 'You are beautiful by day, but in the night you take on an ethereal quality.'

There was an intent look in his eyes, and Sam tried to dispel it by turning his compliment aside with a light rejoinder, but he hardly seemed to hear her, pulling her close against him and whispering endearments in French. 'Oh, *ma mie*,' he said thickly. 'I have tried so hard to be patient. But to see you, to hold you in my arms, and not tell you what you mean to me—I can't stand it any longer. I have to tell you how much I love you, how much I yearn to make you mine. *Chérie*, say that you care for me even a little.'

He was holding her hard against him, his lips raining tiny, passionate kisses on her neck, her throat.

Almost overwhelmed by his urgency, Sam tried to answer him. 'I do like you, Paul, of course I do, but I ...'

But she couldn't go on because he gave a triumphant cry and then kissed her. It was a very expert kiss, and one that left her feeling slightly dazed so that she only slowly became aware that Paul was asking her to marry him. His face thrown into sharp profile by the moon, he looked dashingly handsome, and he was obviously very experienced and sophisticated. He was tall, slim, titled and wealthy, everything a girl could wish for. And Sam was telling herself all this even as she took a step away from him.

Her eyes troubled, she said awkwardly, 'I'm sorry, Paul, but I'm not ...'

Again she wasn't allowed to finish. 'But you're not ready to make up your mind. Ah, forgive me, *chérie*, I know I should have waited longer, given you more time, but you look so lovely tonight.' He bent to kiss her hand, lifting it to his lips. 'But will you promise me to think about my proposal? I know I could make you happy, and you would love my home in France. It would make me the happiest of men to take you there as my bride, my very beautiful bride.' He waited a moment for her to speak but then sighed and said, 'But you are tired. Come, I'll take you home.'

They were silent during the drive home, but as he helped her out of the car at the house, he said again earnestly, '*Chérie*, you did not answer my question; will you promise to think about marrying me?'

Sam flushed a little. 'Yes, of course I will, I could hardly do otherwise.'

'And you will let me know your answer soon? Oh,

I know you think I am rushing you, but if you only knew how much I long to claim you as my promised bride.' He kissed her again then, his lips insinuatingly seeking a response, his hands stroking her caressingly. Abruptly Sam pulled free of his embrace. For a moment she just stood and gazed at him, her breathing unsteady, and then she bade him a hasty goodnight and ran into the house.

She had told the maid not to wait up and she undressed slowly, not bothering to turn on the light, the room was lit far more attractively by the moon rays that shone through the open windows. After she put on her lace-edged nightdress, she didn't go to bed straight away but sat on the windowseat, her legs tucked up so that her chin rested on her knees. So much seemed to have happened today: her clandestine meeting with Mike and all the things he had told her about herself, all of them hateful, and then, when she had faced her father with them, the way he had turned everything round the other way and told her what he knew about Mike. And now Paul had proposed to her. It had certainly been an eventful day, she thought mirthlessly, and not one that she would be able to forget in a hurry. But that did make her give a wry smile; she had been beating her brains out to try to remember her past and now she wanted to forget the present.

Sam gazed miserably out of the window at the shadowed garden and tried to think what was best to do. She had thought that by coming to live with her father she would be safe and happy, but she saw little of him and she could find no happiness in this large, museum-like house. Even so she must have had some kind of life before and she might have been able to find it again if Mike hadn't come storming back into her life and filled her mind with doubts and uncertainties. When she saw the newspaper cutting she had been sure that Mike was the liar and cheat, but now she just didn't know who was telling the truth, who really cared about her, Mike or her father. Or perhaps neither of them really cared about her, perhaps they were both trying to use her to gain their own ends. That thought made her feel worse than ever, and, as always when she tried to concentrate hard, her head began to throb and the familiar pain came back.

Closing her eyes, she leant back against the wall. She felt like a candle in the wind, blown first one way and then the other. Did neither of them care what they were doing to her? Mike so insistent that she was his wife but with not one shred of proof, and her father who so suavely and cleverly refuted every accusation and who wanted her to marry Paul. The thought of Paul made her remember their stroll along the beach, the things he'd said. Sam glanced across at the necklace, lying on the dressing-table in a shimmering heap; if he was wealthy enough to give her a present like that then he couldn't be interested in her just for her money. And he'd said he wanted to take her to France, to live in his house there. And suddenly she saw this as a way of escape. If she married Paul he would take her far away from Barbados, away from Mike and her father, she wouldn't be torn apart by doubt and uncertainty any more, she would be able to create a new life for herself where she could shut out all the bitter memories.

But how could she possibly marry a man just to escape from a situation that was becoming unbearable? To do so would be a supreme act of selfishness, and she hadn't sunk quite that low, not yet. But how else was she to break free? If she tried to leave she was quite sure that her father would bring her back; he would of course explain that it was for her own good, that she might be kidnapped again, but she would be brought back all the same. And Paul had said that he loved her, surely then she needn't feel guilty if she married him without loving him in return. He would have what he wanted and she liked him a lot, perhaps it was just too soon for her to love him. But even as she tried to find plausible reasons for marrying Paul, at the back of her mind there was a nagging doubt about his proposal. The perfect setting of the moonlight on the water, the palm trees sighing in the breeze—it had all been too contrived somehow. And when he had kissed her, it had been technique more than desire. He had used his expertise to overwhelm her, confident of his ability to make her respond, and for a while it had worked, but now, unbidden, her mind filled with the memory of Mike's kisses, the urgency that had brooked no denial, his need for her that had forced a response that lifted them both to the heights of passion. Even the touch of his hand had electrified her and made her physically aware of him as she had never been with Paul.

Sam turned dejectedly away from the window and got into bed. But Mike was a criminal, a drop-out who couldn't take the pace of ordinary life and who now spent his time bumming around the West Indies, lying and cheating to get money. And no way could she live with a man like that. Better to marry a man she didn't love than to be used and degraded.

The noise of the phone ringing woke Sam the next morning and she realised that she had slept very late, the sun already high in the sky. Yawningly she picked up the receiver.

'Miss Ashby? This is Rosetta's Boutique in Bridgetown. The clothes you ordered have arrived. I'm sorry they took so long, but we had difficulty in obtaining exactly what you wanted and some of the garments had to be specially made.'

'I'm sorry,' Sam tried to gather her wits together, 'I'm afraid I don't quite remember.'

The woman's voice went on. 'Well, it was some time ago. Before you were kidnapped. I'll describe the clothes to you.'

She started going into detail about colours and styles and presently Sam heard a click on the line as if someone had replaced a receiver. Immediately the woman's tone altered and she said, 'Hold on a moment, please.' Then Mike's voice came on. 'Hallo, Sam.'

'Mike! But why all this rigmarole about clothes?'

'Sorry, sweetheart, but I've tried to phone you dozens of times and your father's secretary always intercepts the calls, so I got the operator at the hotel to help me with this subterfuge. How are you?'

'I'm—I'm fine. How's your head?'

'I'll live. Listen, Sam, I have to talk to you.'

'No. We've said everything there is to say between us.'

'Oh no, we haven't. Not by a long shot,' he said grimly. 'We have to meet soon. I'm going to the harbour now and I'll anchor off the cove below your father's place in half an hour. Get there as soon as you can and try not to have anyone follow you.'

Her voice sharp with indignation, Sam said, 'You

can't order me around like that, Mike. I'm not going to meet you and that's final!'

His tone hardened. 'Then I shall just have to come up to the house and find you,' and he put down the phone.

Sam stared at the receiver in her hand resentfully. How dared he speak to her as if he had the right to order her around. If he thought she would meet him after yesterday, he was crazy! She lay mutinously back on the pillows for a few minutes but then got reluctantly out of bed. She knew Mike well enough to know that if he said he'd do something then he would keep his word, even if it was something crazy like coming up to the house to find her when he knew that her father's men would throw him out again.

Putting on an orange towelling bikini with a matching beach robe, Sam picked up her bathing cap and made her way to the back stairs. There didn't seem to be any one about, although she could hear the hum of an electric polisher being used on the parquet flooring somewhere downstairs. Slipping out of a side door, she made sure the coast was clear and then ran behind a screen of shrubs that hid her from the house. So far so good, now all she had to do was to avoid the guards that patrolled the walls. But even this was easier than she had thought and soon she was running down through the woodland to the cove, confident that she hadn't been seen. She waited in the shade of the trees until she saw the boat come along and anchor in the bay as it had before and then she put on her cap, hid her robe beneath some leaves, and swam swiftly out to the raft. She had hardly reached it and pulled off the cap to shake her hair loose before she saw Mike cutting through the water towards her. He wasn't wearing the air-tanks this time and was swimming on the surface.

He caught hold of the raft and shook the water from his face. 'Were you followed?'

Sam shook her head. 'No, I'm sure I wasn't.'

'Good.' He lifted himself with one heave of his powerful arms and swung up to sit beside her.

She started to say, 'What did you want?' and then stopped as his eyes went over her and grew dark. He reached out for her, and even as she started to protest he bore her back against the hardness of the raft, his mouth finding hers and imprisoning it fiercely, kissing her with a kind of savagery, like a man too long denied.

At last he raised his head, his breathing unsteady. She had stopped resisting him, her lips were open and her eyes closed. He could feel her heart beating fast under his moving hand. He leant his weight against her, pinning her against the raft. The muscles holding her down were steel knots, and yet for all his strength he hadn't hurt her. He said raggedly, 'Oh, Sam, I need you. I need you so much.'

Opening her eyes, she stared up at him. The desire for her was still there in his eyes. A wave of sensuality grew in her and her skin was on fire where it touched his. His caressing hand made her want to move against him, to touch him, but then she turned her head aside and said abruptly, 'Why did you want to see me? Just for this?'

'No, not for this.' His voice was harsh, bitter almost, and he lifted his weight off her. 'You can't do it, Sam. I'm not going to let you.'

She looked at him in bewilderment, then sat up and

adjusted the straps of her bikini. 'Do what? What are you talking about?'

'Don't pretend you don't know. It's all over this morning's papers.'

'What is? Mike, will you please explain? I don't know what you're talking about.'

He looked at her searchingly for a moment and then said, 'God, I don't believe you do.' Then, 'Haven't you seen today's paper?'

'No, I was still in bed when you phoned.' She looked at him in puzzlement. 'Why, what does it say?'

Bluntly he answered, 'That you and de Lacey are to be married. And that the match does, of course, have your father's full approval.'

Sam gasped. 'But—but that isn't true! I didn't say I would, I only said that I ...' She broke off as Mike's hand gripped her wrist.

'He has asked you, then?'

'Yes, last night. But how could the papers possibly know? It must be just a rumour they picked up.'

Mike's mouth set into a thin line. 'Possibly, although the story was pretty definite. Perhaps it just anticipated the truth. But you can't marry him, Sam.'

Immediately her eyes flashed as resentment grew in her. 'Why shouldn't I marry him if I want to?'

He jerked her suddenly towards him and his face was very close to hers, his eyes angry. 'Because bigamy is a criminal offence, that's why not!'

Sam glared back at him. 'And what do you call kidnapping? No matter how often you say it, Mike, I shall never believe that I was really married to you. And I like Paul, if I want to marry him I shall go ahead and do it.'

His tone grew contemptuous. 'You'd marry a man you don't love?'

Raising her eyes, Sam looked straight into his. 'I lived with you and I didn't love you. Where's the difference?'

He flinched as if she'd hit him and went pale under his tan. After a moment he said, 'He's just a fortune-hunter, a gigolo, if you like. And he certainly isn't good enough for you,' he added forcefully.

Sam laughed aloud. 'And you? What are you? Nothing but a beachcomber, a drop-out who couldn't stand the pace and went native. Do you seriously think that I should choose you instead of Paul?'

For a moment she thought she'd gone too far as a look of almost primitive savagery came into his eyes, but then his jaw tautened and he dropped her wrist.

'So your father's been talking about me, has he?'

'It was only fair. You said some pretty foul things about him,' Sam reminded him.

Mike looked at her for a moment before saying with a shrug, 'Okay. But let's get things in perspective. Maybe I am a drop-out in your father's eyes, but only because I don't want to be a success by his standards. Yes, I had my own business and it was doing well, really well. I'd raised it to be the top in that particular field and I'd started to take over smaller rivals, put them out of business. But then one day I went to visit a plant I'd taken over on the day it closed down and I saw the men coming out. It was an old-established firm that hadn't modernised enough and some of the men had been there for thirty or forty years. Some of them had tears in their eyes as they came out of the factory gates. Grown men crying, Sam! And it was then I realised the kind of man I was turning into. Someone with an ambition so ruthless that he didn't care who he trod on on the way to the top. Someone like your father,' he added deliberately. 'And I decided there and then that no way was I going on like that. It was a financial dunghill, and I didn't want to be the cock crowing at the top of it. So the next day I opened that firm again and arranged for it to be gradually brought up to date, and then I appointed someone to take over the directorship of my company, but tied up in such a way that they couldn't expand by taking over other firms, only by creating new products; that way nobody gets hurt.'

'You gave your company away?' Sam's voice was incredulous.

'No, I didn't give it away, it's still mine and I can draw as much money as I want from it. I'm still a fairly rich man, if that's what's worrying you. But I decided to come out here for a year to think things through, to find myself again, if you like, and I fell in love with the place and decided to stay. I had my boat and could go when and where I pleased. I'm happy in that I need nothing that others feel essential: big houses, cars, possessions.' He paused. 'Or at least I was contented until you came along.' He turned to look at her directly. 'But then everything changed. I wanted to put the world at your feet.' His mouth twisted into a wry grimace. 'But you already had the world, your father had given you far more of it than I ever could. But then a very wonderful thing happened.' His eyes met hers and held them. 'You said that you felt the same way I did. That you'd had enough of being a pawn in your father's power game and that you just wanted to leave it all behind you and join me on the boat, just sailing anywhere in the world we wanted to go.'

'For always?' Sam asked a little unsteadily.

'No, not for always,' he said gently. 'Just until the scars had healed on all your wounds. Then we were going to settle down somewhere, have kids, be just like any other married couple.' Softly he added, 'And that's what I still want, Sam, very much.'

For a few minutes she gazed at him, her eyes shadowed by uncertainty, then she put her head in her hands and shook it from side to side. 'Oh, Mike, if only I could believe you! If only I could be sure you were speaking the truth.'

Urgently he said, 'I am, Sam. I swear it.'

He tried to put his arms round her, but she pulled away and stood up. 'No, don't touch me. I can't even think straight when you're near me.' She said agitatedly, 'I should never have come here, never have listened to you. When I'm with you I want to believe you, but then Daddy tells me that you're lying and I want to believe him.' She put her hands up to her throbbing temples, her voice rising in distress. 'Can't you see what you're doing to me? You're tearing me apart between you. You're both trying to force a decision on me that I don't want to make.'

Tears began to pour down her cheeks and this time she was unable to push him away when he put his arms round her. 'Oh, Mike, help me! Please help me,' she sobbed.

She had been speaking so loudly and he had been so intent on comforting her that neither of them heard the motor boat approaching the raft until it was almost up to them. There were three of her father's men in it and one pointed a gun at Mike while another held the boat steady against the raft with a heavy wooden boathook. The third jumped on to the raft and pulled Sam away from Mike, who could only stand there, grim-faced, the gun still pointing at his chest.

There was nothing Sam could do, she could only let herself be helped into the boat and turn to look miserably at Mike. But then she saw the man with the gun lower it to the level of Mike's knee-cap and his finger tighten on the trigger. Sam screamed and made a wild lunge for his arm. The gun went off and the man let out an obscene epithet as it was knocked out of his hand into the sea. Out of the corner of her eye she saw Mike make a grab for her, but then the man with the boat-hook swung it up to try and stop him, aiming it wildly. Mike ducked and then the boathook hit Sam on the side of the head with such force that she was knocked backwards into the water.

The blow hadn't knocked her out completely, but she was only semi-conscious and quite incapable of anything but a token effort to get to the surface. The bottom seemed a long way down and she swallowed water before she even reached it. Dazedly she tried to push herself off the coral rocks, but her head was so muzzy that she fell back again, her chest bursting. But then she was being lifted towards the surface, strong arms holding her securely as Mike's powerful muscles carried them through the water as she fought for breath. Their heads broke the surface at last and he held her as she coughed and choked, gasping the blessed air.

Then the power boat had come alongside them and she felt herself lifted into it before it immediately turned and headed for the shore, leaving Mike alone in the sea. Helplessly he watched and then turned to swim to his own boat.

One of the men carried her nearly all the way back to the house, but when they were almost there she insisted on getting down. 'I'm all right now. I can manage.'

He looked relieved and let her go. She reeled as if she was drunk at first and was grateful for the banister to hang on to going up the stairs. Her room was empty, the bed made, and she collapsed on to it, regardless of her wet swimsuit. Her head was a riot of flashing colours against a black void and she had to clench her teeth to stop herself from crying out with pain. It seemed to take a very long time for the pain to go away and for the colours to subside, and afterwards she just lay on the bed feeling drained and exhausted. Confused pictures started coming into her mind then, pictures of people, places, events, and then suddenly they all dovetailed together and became clear in her mind. Sam turned over and gazed at the ceiling, knowing that everything was all right and she saw her way clear ahead. It was a very wonderful feeling, and one that she lay and savoured for quite some time before she briskly swung her legs to the ground and went to find herself some clothes.

She chose a pair of white denims and a red halterneck sun-top and dressed quickly. Then she picked up the phone and dialled Paul's number. He answered almost immediately and she asked him to come round to the house straight away.

'You are going to give me your decision?' he said eagerly. 'But, *ma mie*, why can you not tell me over the phone? It is cruel of you to keep me in suspense like this.'

But she merely said, 'Just come, Paul, quickly,' and

he promised to be there in ten minutes.

Sam turned to her mirror to put on some make-up and paused, staring at her reflection. Her eyes were bright with eagerness and her face seemed to have come alive. Almost reverently she raised a hand to her cheek. Could love really transform her like this? Then she blinked and hurried to apply her make-up before Paul arrived. She heard a car outside and saw her own red sports car that Paul had been using coming up the driveway. Quickly she scooped up the diamond and emerald necklace and put it into her handbag and ran downstairs to meet him.

He was waiting for her in the hall and she took his arm and went to draw him outside again, but Mrs Gregory was there too and stepped towards her.

'Miss Ashby, I think you might want this. It was in the pocket of one of your jackets that had been sent to be cleaned.' She handed her an envelope and as Sam took it she noticed a gleam of malice in the older woman's eyes.

Calmly Sam said, 'Thank you, Mrs Gregory. Will you tell my father that I won't be in to dinner?' And she gave a small smile as she tucked the envelope unopened into her bag and saw the baffled look on the house-keeper's face.

Turning back to Paul, Sam smiled at him. 'Let's go for a drive, shall we? Up the Platinum Coast?'

Paul returned the smile confidently, sure that she was going to accept his proposal. But he had driven only a mile or so along the coast road before Sam asked him to pull into the forecourt of an hotel.

'Here?' he asked in surprise.

'Yes, please. Because this is where I'm getting out.'

He turned to her in astonishment and Sam said baldly, 'I'm not going to marry you, Paul. Thanks for the offer, but I'm in love with someone else. So I brought this to give back to you.' She opened her bag and took out the necklace. It lay in her hands, the sun reflecting off it so brilliantly that it hurt her eyes. 'It's very beautiful and I shall always remember that you wanted me to have it, but I don't need that kind of thing, not any more.'

She pushed the necklace towards him, but the shock in his eyes suddenly faded and his mouth twisted. 'Then you had better give it back to your father,' he said bitterly. 'It was he who bought it and gave it to me to pass on to you.'

Sam's eyes widened. 'You mean there was no ancestress from the court of Marie Antoinette?'

Paul shrugged and spread his hands expressively. 'What would you? It made everything much more romantic, did it not?' He glanced at the necklace. 'The cost of that would restore my home and put my estates in good heart again so that they would provide enough for me to live on.' His voice grew even more bitter. 'Enough so that I didn't have to travel the world looking for a rich heiress. I could go home and marry the girl I ...' He broke off abruptly. 'I beg your pardon, I had not meant to say that to you. It is not your fault that you do not care for me. I must not have tried hard enough.' He passed a hand rather wearily over his face.

Sam said slowly, 'My father said you were very well connected?'

'Oh, I am. To many members of the nobility who are all as poor as I, all struggling to hold their heritage together against taxes and inflation. I suppose I'm lucky, I do at least have myself to sell even if all the other treasures have gone.' He made an effort and pulled himself together. 'But that is my problem. I wish you joy with this man you love, *chérie*. You deserve it, you are *une fille très belle*. Tell me, was it because your father insisted on giving news of our engagement to the press before you actually said yes that turned you against me? I was afraid it might, but he wouldn't listen.'

Sam shook her head. 'No, it wasn't that. It was just —well, I suppose I came to my senses again.'

'Well, he is a very lucky man. Have you told your father yet?'

She smiled slightly. 'As a matter of fact I haven't told the man himself yet. That's why I asked you to bring me to this hotel. He's staying here.'

Paul's eyebrows flew up in astonishment. 'Then I had better bow out of your life. If he saw us together he might get the wrong idea.' He took the car keys out of the ignition and gave them to her. 'You'd better take these.'

He turned to get out of the car, but Sam impulsively put a hand on his arm. 'Paul, wait a minute.' She smiled at him. 'I'd like to give *you* a wedding present.'

'Me? But I'm not getting married,' he exclaimed.

'But if I gave you this, couldn't you hurry home to that girl you left behind in France?' Again she held out the necklace to him. 'Please take it, Paul, you'd be doing me a big favour and I'd very much like you to have it.' She laughed. 'After all, you do deserve *some* reward for all that hard work you put in on me.' And before he could recover from his open-mouthed astonishment she stuffed the necklace into his pocket. 'Goodbye, Paul, have a safe journey home.'

Quickly she got out of the car and ran across to the

entrance of the Hotel Miramar without a backward glance.

The foyer was busy with a coachload of incoming travellers and she had to wait impatiently for a few minutes before she could attract the receptionist's attention.

'You have a Mr Scott staying here—Mike Scott. Could you contact him for me, please?'

The receptionist consulted his register and then shook his head. 'I'm sorry, but Mr Scott has already checked out.'

'Checked out?' Sam stared at him in disbelief.

'That's right, madam. He left this morning after booking a seat on the two-thirty plane to London.'

Hastily Sam glanced at her watch. Almost two o'clock, and the airport was on the other side of Bridgetown! Without stopping to think, she ran out of the hotel and down the steps looking wildly round for a taxi. Usually there were plenty outside the hotels, but now, of course, there wasn't one in sight. Oh no, she just had to get to the airport in time! And then she saw her sports car parked under the trees and remembered that Paul had given her the keys. Quickly she pulled them out of her bag and got into the car, her hands fumbling at the controls in her haste. But then, thankfully, it started and she was swinging back on to the coast road and heading for Bridgetown. At first she was so frightened that she held the wheel terribly tightly, her hands wet with perspiration. The engine started to scream as she went faster until she dared to take one hand off the wheel and change gear. But after that she regained some of her confidence and it became easier, and when she reached Bridgetown she was able to dart in and out of the slower traffic and keep her hand on the horn to clear a way through the pedestrians who seemed to enjoy strolling down the middle of the road.

For a few hellishly frustrating minutes she was held up by a delivery van in Trafalgar Square, but then she was crossing Chamberlain Bridge over a river thick with boats and accelerating along Bay Street towards Highway Seven and the airport. The next few miles were covered with her foot fully down on the accelerator, regardless of speed limits, and she skidded to a stop outside the departure building at exactly two-twenty. Leaving the car door wide, she ran inside and up to the British Airways desk.

'The two-thirty flight to London,' she gasped.

'I'm sorry, but you're too late, it's already boarded. You'll have to take the next flight,' the pretty ground receptionist told her.

'No, you don't understand,' Sam said desperately. 'I have to get a message to someone on the plane. Oh, please, it's most terribly urgent,' she pleaded.

'Well, I don't know. Just a moment.' The girl disappeared into an office behind her while Sam gripped the edge of the desk hard, willing her to hurry.

Presently the girl came out with a man in uniform who looked Sam over rather suspiciously. 'You say you want to get a message to someone on the plane?'

'Yes. It's terribly important. Oh, please hurry.'

He must have read her distress in her face because his expression changed and he said briskly, 'All right, I'll see what I can do. What's the name of the passenger?'

'Scott. Mike Scott.'

'And the message?'

For a second Sam hesitated, but then she said firmly, 'Will you just tell him that his wife is here?'

The man gave her a quick glance, then nodded and went back into his office. He seemed to be gone for ages. Sam paced up and down, waiting, unable to stand still. Then above her head she heard the roar of a big jet taking off and running to a window she saw a plane with British Airways insignia climbing high into the sky. So she had been too late after all. She stood there hopelessly, staring at the plane as it climbed ever higher into the cloudless blue of the sky.

Tears of frustration and despair came into Sam's eyes and she groped in her bag for a handkerchief. Her fingers fumbled on the envelope Mrs Gregory had given her and she slowly drew it out. Inside was a photograph, the type that street photographers take, and it showed her and Mike walking along a road near the harbour together. Mike had his arm possessively across her shoulders and they were looking into each other's eyes oblivious to everyone else. Sam felt an almost physical pain as she looked at it. She had wanted proof that she had known Mike for so long and now it had been casually handed to her. Given with malice and self-interest at heart, of course, and given too late. If only she'd had it just a few hours earlier! Again she looked up at the plane that was now no bigger than a toy.

Then she felt a touch on her arm and turned lifelessly to find the uniformed man behind her. He smiled at her and pointed to some doors. 'If you go through there you shouldn't have long to wait.'

Sam looked up at him stupidly. 'To wait? But I don't understand, the plane's gone.'

'Yes, but we got the message through in time. Mr Scott should be along at any moment.'

Her face changing from despair to incredulous joy, Sam could only gaze up at him speechlessly. He grinned and turned away and then Sam was running towards the doors he'd indicated. They opened on to a windowed corridor above the airport concourse, but there were three side corridors opening off it and she didn't know which one to take, so she had to just stand there, bursting with impatience, and ready to run to him the moment he came in sight.

But when Mike did turn a corner at the end of a long corridor, she found that she couldn't move. He was dressed in a dark business suit more suited to the English climate than the West Indies and he carried a briefcase in his hand. As soon as he saw her he stopped dead so that the uniformed official who was accompanying him almost bumped into him. He stood and stared at her as if he couldn't really believe his own eyes. Then slowly, almost as if he were in a dream, he began to walk along the corridor, but after a few steps his pace began to quicken and then suddenly he was running and Sam found herself rushing to meet him. Mike dropped his briefcase and swept her into his arms, lifting her off her feet and holding her so tightly that she could hardly breathe.

'Oh, Sam. Sam.' He said her name over and over again, his face buried in her hair.

Sam had her arms tight round his neck, laughing and crying at the same time. And then, regardless of their surroundings, she said fervently, 'Oh, Mike, I love you so much!'

He set her down on her feet and cupped her face in

his hands. For a moment he looked at her, drinking in every detail of her rapturous face, her eyes alight with love, then he lowered his head to kiss her hard on the mouth.

A discreet cough made them draw apart at last and they turned somewhat dazedly to find the official grinning at them. 'I hate to break it up,' he smiled, 'but a planeload of people will be coming along here in just a few minutes.' He handed Mike his briefcase and then opened the doors for them to go back into the main building.

Mike held out his hand to her and Sam put hers into his big one. It felt very warm and strong as it closed tightly over hers. They walked through the airport and out on to the steps. Mike gave his head a little shake and then grinned at her.

'Something tells me I'm not going to come down to earth for quite some time. How did you get here?'

'In my sports car. It's over there,' she pointed.

'You came in that?'

'Yes, I remembered how to drive it.'

He glanced at her quickly but then took the keys from her and drove away from the airport. They didn't say much as they drove along and Sam didn't bother to ask where they were going, she was too full of happiness, too thankful that Mike was beside her to care. She sat very close to him, her shoulder against his, and he turned often to look at her, as if he still couldn't quite believe she was really there.

At length he pulled up outside an old brick plantation house that lay well back off the road. Climbing plants rioted up the walls and the gardens were full of flowers lifting their heads to the sun. But inside it was cool and an elderly man smiled a welcome to this small hotel away from the tourist track. He led them upstairs to a circular-shaped room with long windows wide open to the soft breeze and then left them alone.

For a moment they looked at each other, suddenly awkward, then Mike fished in his inside pocket and held something out to her. 'Here, you'd better put this on. I bought it for you our last day in St Vincent and had it engraved.'

It was a wedding ring, very simple and plain. Slowly Sam took it from him and turned it to read the inscription. It said 'Mike and Sam—always'. She made a little choking sound and Mike reached out and put the ring on her finger.

'Oh, Sam. Oh, God, if you only knew how much I've missed you!'

He took her in his arms and held her close. He didn't kiss her but just let her feel his strength about her. Comfort, tenderness, safety. His love enveloped her. Gently he stroked her hair, but presently, when she had stopped trembling, he put her a little way away from him and said, 'When did you remember?'

'Remember?'

'Get your memory back. Was it the blow on the head that did it?'

Sam looked at him wide-eyed. 'Is that why you think I came back to you?' She reached up to touch his face. 'No, Mike, I still can't remember anything that happened before I woke up on the dinghy. I don't suppose I ever will now.' She gave a ghost of a smile. 'But perhaps that blow on the head did at least knock some sense into me. It made me realise that I loved you and that I wanted to spend the rest of my life with you. I'd been so mixed up—and then everything suddenly became very clear. And you were right about Paul, he was just a fortune-hunter, but a nice one. You were right about everything, and I was a fool not to realise it all along. I'm sorry, Mike. I ruined what we had. You must have given up on me completely to go back to England.' She looked away unhappily, but turned quickly back when he laughed.

'Don't you know me well enough yet to realise that I wouldn't give up so easily? I was going to England to find the priest who married us and bring him back here to testify to our marriage. To stop your father deliberately letting you commit bigamy and also to convince you once and for all that we're married, and I'm not a rapist as you once called me.'

Sam hung her head. 'I'm sorry, Mike,' she said meekly.

He tilted up her chin. 'You did turn out to be a very willing victim.' Lowering his head, he kissed her very gently, very tenderly, and then looked into her eyes. 'But this time we're going to do it my way, Sam. The notice of our marriage will be put in the papers for all the world to see. And your father can either accept me or not, it won't make any difference. There'll be no more hiding, no more running away, do you understand?'

For answer she put her arms round his neck and kissed him long and lingeringly. When she drew away from him he immediately pulled her back, but Sam moved her head away before he could kiss her and said, 'Mike, do you think you could find our island again?'

He smiled. 'I have it charted down to the last detail. And I have my eye on another boat that would suit us perfectly until we decide exactly where we want to settle down.'

He went to kiss her again, but she moved away and said rather teasingly, 'Are you really well off, Mike?'

His eyebrows rose quizzically and he looked amused. 'I suppose you could say that. Why?'

'Because I didn't bring anything with me. I came to you just as I am. I shall need a whole new wardrobe of clothes before we leave Barbados.'

He grinned. 'And I left my suitcase on the plane. It must be halfway to London by now. We'll have to go out later and buy what we need.'

Sam began to unbutton his jacket and slip it off his shoulders. 'Later?'

His hands tightened on her waist. 'Well, perhaps to-morrow.'

She undid his tie and dropped it on the floor, then began to unbutton his shirt.

'Better make it a couple of days,' he said, his voice suddenly uneven.

Slowly Sam took off his shirt and ran her fingers lightly over his chest, then bent to kiss him.

'We'll make that next week,' he said firmly, and picked her up to carry her to the sun-dappled bed.